The Legend of the Inn at Maiden Falls...

There are lots of rumors, but no one is exactly sure why even the crankiest twosomes get so very coosome when they spend time at the historic Inn at Maiden Falls, nestled in the Colorado Rockies. Maybe it's the beautiful vista of all that rushing water (the falls) outside the windows. Maybe it's the clean, invigorating mountain air stirring up their blood. Or maybe (as the whispers say) there really are lusty ghosts of shady ladies past floating around the rafters. Old-timers say the inn was a famous brothel more than a hundred years ago; all the "soiled doves" may have mysteriously passed away, but their spirits remain to help young lovers discover the joy of sensual pleasure. Or so the story goes...

Dear Reader,

I really enjoy working with other writers. And I couldn't ask for more creative people to work with than Colleen Collins and Heather MacAllister. When we brainstormed ideas for a miniseries, it's my recollection that Colleen came up with the concept of an old bordello now turned into a hotel, I added the ghosts of good-time girls from the past hanging around the rafters, and Heather upped the comedy and the spice when she suggested we make it a *honeymoon* hotel, with sassy, saucy ghosts assigned to help the new brides and grooms rev up their sex lives. And so THE SPIRITS ARE WILLING trilogy was born.

I piped up right away and claimed dibs on a ghost as my heroine rather than just a secondary character, and bless their hearts, they let me get away with it! I've written books with a leprechaun, a hero with superpowers, Santa Claus, and a couple of sweet old ladies who thought they were witches, but this is my first ghost heroine. I hope you enjoy meeting Rose, a smart, impetuous woman who just happens to be stuck in the wrong place at the very worst time and is the least experienced fallen woman. When she sees Ned, he's a big temptation for a woman who hasn't been kissed in 109 years.

If you find the idea of a willing spirit a whole lot of fun, you're in the right place!

Julie Kistler

Books by Julie Kistler

HARLEQUIN TEMPTATION
957—HOT PROSPECT*
961—CUT TO THE CHASE*
965—PACKING HEAT*

*The True Blue Calhouns

JULIE KISTLER

IT'S IN HIS KISS

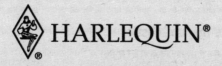

HARLEQUIN®

TORONTO • NEW YORK • LONDON
AMSTERDAM • PARIS • SYDNEY • HAMBURG
STOCKHOLM • ATHENS • TOKYO • MILAN • MADRID
PRAGUE • WARSAW • BUDAPEST • AUCKLAND

To Colleen and Heather,
the most fun writing partners ever!

ISBN 0-373-69185-8

IT'S IN HIS KISS

Copyright © 2004 by Julie Kistler.

This edition published by arrangement with Harlequin Books S.A.

® and TM are trademarks of the publisher. Trademarks indicated with
® are registered in the United States Patent and Trademark Office, the
Canadian Trade Marks Office and in other countries.

www.eHarlequin.com

Printed in U.S.A.

The Golden Rules for Miss Arlotta's Girls

We know rules are not your favorite things,
but some things need to be written down.
So here's your Golden Rules, girls. Abide by 'em
and we'll all do just fine. We weren't exactly angels
when we were here the first time around,
but we've got another chance. So we want to do what
we can to keep the idea of holy matrimony satisfying
so's nobody's man will be tempted to go lookin'
elsewhere for a good time. It may not seem fair,
but them's the rules. We helped 'em stray.
Now we're helping 'em stay.

Rule #1: You will never, ever do anything that might
come between the bride and groom.

Rule #2: No visibility. You can't be scarin'
the livin' daylights out of folks by fading in
and out or showing up in bits and pieces
at the wrong time.

Rule #3: Never, ever make love
with a guest yourself.
No exceptions.

Rule #4: No emotional attachments to
anyone. You can't follow them when they
leave, so you might as well not get attached.

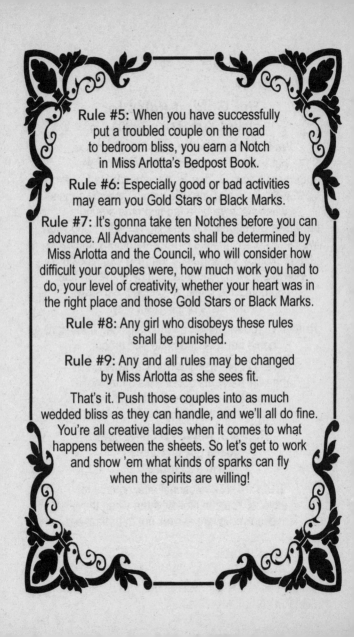

Rule #5: When you have successfully put a troubled couple on the road to bedroom bliss, you earn a Notch in Miss Arlotta's Bedpost Book.

Rule #6: Especially good or bad activities may earn you Gold Stars or Black Marks.

Rule #7: It's gonna take ten Notches before you can advance. All Advancements shall be determined by Miss Arlotta and the Council, who will consider how difficult your couples were, how much work you had to do, your level of creativity, whether your heart was in the right place and those Gold Stars or Black Marks.

Rule #8: Any girl who disobeys these rules shall be punished.

Rule #9: Any and all rules may be changed by Miss Arlotta as she sees fit.

That's it. Push those couples into as much wedded bliss as they can handle, and we'll all do fine. You're all creative ladies when it comes to what happens between the sheets. So let's get to work and show 'em what kinds of sparks can fly when the spirits are willing!

Prologue

A Sunday in June
Maiden Falls, Colorado, 1895

ROSE ELIZABETH TATE was furious. It had been hours since she'd had that terrible argument with her father, slammed a few articles of clothing and some of her favorite books into a suitcase, spirited herself out through the servants' quarters of the Tate mansion and boarded the train. Now here she was in Maiden Falls, still shaking with anger. But it was too late to turn back now. All she could do was put one foot in front of the other.

Dragging her heavy suitcase along the wooden sidewalk, Rose stopped for a moment to get her bearings. Maiden Falls didn't look like much, did it?

"Who cares?" she asked no one in particular. "So the town looks a little seedy. Who cares?"

After all, she was a girl of the nineties and she could chart her own course, without her father's help or interference. Or anyone else's! And that included that cad, Edmund Mulgrew. Edmund might've stolen her virtue, but he could never kill her spirit.

"Stolen my virtue," she said self-righteously, poking into her pocket for her wire-rimmed spectacles so that at least she could see where she was going. "Poppycock! I'm still plenty virtuous."

As Rose began her search for a carriage to take her away from the dilapidated shack Maiden Falls called a train station, one of the ostrich plumes on her darling new hat drooped right in front of her eyeglasses. She suddenly realized that this might be the last new hat she'd have for some time.

"I'll be fine," she said bravely, ripping the feather off completely. "Fine! Once I'm working for Miss Arlotta, grateful men will be vying for my favors, competing against each other to give me every little thing my heart desires. Why, I'll have a thousand beautiful hats."

Mentioning the notorious Miss Arlotta earned her a strange look from a nasty man with a large mustache, but Rose ignored him. If she was really going to be a soiled dove, then she'd have to get used to disapproval, wouldn't she?

She peered at the man with the mustache. He certainly wasn't anyone important. Who cared what he thought, anyway?

After all, Father had already told her in no uncertain terms that she was ruined. So she would embrace that ruination, marching into her future as a fallen maiden with her head held high. "After Edmund, what other choice do I have?"

Edmund. It was galling to admit that her father had been right all along about him. But it wasn't her fault. How was she supposed to know she couldn't trust his sweet words and even sweeter kisses? How was she supposed to know that enjoying those kisses was wrong when it felt so right?

How was she supposed to know that a man who

made you swoon might still not be a good man? Just very good at making you swoon.

She'd honestly never guessed it would be like that, and she had read every "sensation" novel written by Mary Elizabeth Braddon and every dime novel by Laura Jean Libbey. They were wonderful books, full of passion and adventure and romance, but they told you straight out that the kisses of a bad man would taste like poison. As Rose now knew, that was a lie. Edmund's heart might be black, but his kisses were... wonderful.

"It's all Father's fault," she maintained. "If he'd only let me see Edmund in the clear light of day, I'd never have fallen for all the lies. I'd never have fallen under his spell. I'd never have..."

Fallen. Not that it made any difference at this point. Those few tempestuous liaisons had ruined her reputation. Now that both her father and her lover had washed their hands of her, she had two choices—to become a strumpet out in the open or the equivalent of a nun, cloistered in her father's mansion, forcibly denied any contact with sinful books, diverting entertainments or interesting men.

She'd made up her mind today, after that last argument with her father. She'd decided to become a strumpet.

"Excuse me, sir," she said brightly to the man with the nasty mustache, who was still hovering at her elbow. "Is there any sort of carriage I can hire to take me to Miss Arlotta's establishment?"

He cocked an eyebrow at her, narrowly missing her shiny patent leather boot as he shot a stream of tobacco out the side of his mouth. "You want to git to Miss Ar-lotty's? What fer?"

"I don't think that's any of your concern. I simply…" She brought down her chin a notch. "Are there any carriages around here or not?"

"Not. Everybody here walks on the two feet God gave 'em. Unless they got a horse. Which I ain't and you don't." With an unpleasant expression twisting his features, he ambled off, leaving Rose alone in the dust. But she jumped and almost fell off the boardwalk when a scruffy boy popped up behind her.

"Miss Arlotta's is that way," he offered shyly, crooking his dirty thumb toward the end of the street. "All the way to the edge of town."

"Thank you," Rose said politely. "I don't suppose I could offer you a penny to carry my bag, could I? It's very heavy."

He ducked his head. "I'm afraid not, ma'am. I ain't allowed to go by Miss Arlotta's. My ma says all the ladies there is painted. And dirty. Like the Queen of Sheba. And I ain't to look at them, not even when they parade through town, all fancied-up, headed for their Sunday picnic down by the Falls. Ma says we should look the other way, just so they're clear how much we don't like 'em."

"Whatever are you talking about?" she asked.

"If you're here next Sunday, you'll see," he said hastily. "They already done it today, but I reckon they'll go again next Sunday right about noontime. But remember, if you see 'em, keep your head down and sneer." After that last bizarre warning, the boy ran off.

"Keep my head down and sneer. I don't think so."

Rose lifted her bulky suitcase in both hands and headed in the direction he'd indicated. "Who cares what that child's mother thinks of the ladies at Miss Arlotta's? She probably resents them for having nice clothes and jewels, and for all the fun they're having!"

She was dusty and tired by the time she'd finally dragged her bag to the edge of town, but her spirit was unbowed. Her mood improved considerably when the dirt and dust gave way to a green, grassy lawn enclosed by a high, wrought-iron fence. A wooden sign, flapping against the fence, read Miss Arlotta's Social Club.

Why, the house was positively lovely. It wasn't just the delicate gingerbread wrapped around the big house's Queen Anne curves or the pretty turret or the porch flanking the entire roof. No, what impressed her the most was that the house was pink. Pink! How very cheery.

As she let herself in through the gate and marched up the stairs to the front door, ready to grasp the shiny brass knocker, Rose took a deep breath. She didn't want to faint dead away on the steps of a bawdy house, but she was definitely feeling skittish with nerves and excitement. She was determined to embrace this new, wicked life, and there was no turning back now. As she raised her hand to the knocker, the door suddenly swung open from inside. A large man wearing a bowler hat appeared in the opening.

"Hullo, ma'am," he said gruffly. "Guess you're lookin' for work."

"Why, yes, I—" She broke off. "Is it that obvious?"

She didn't think she looked like a scarlet woman, all things considered. Not yet, anyway.

"You've got baggage. I know what that means. You'll have to come in and see Miss Arlotta. She'll decide whether you're fit for work here."

"I assure you I'm fit," Rose told him as she stepped inside, and the burly man took her satchel from her hand. Good. She was tired of carrying it, and really sorry she'd packed it full of books.

But what a strange place. Even though it was a bright, sunny afternoon outside, it was dark and smoky inside, with heavy red draperies, dripping with golden fringe, pulled tight at all the windows. The walls were dark oak, but trimmed in gilt, with chubby Cupids and curvy figures of Venus swirling around on the ceiling. So this was what a den of iniquity looked like. How exciting!

Rose edged away from her guide, too curious not to peek around the corner into the main parlor, where she could hear voices and music. Everywhere she looked, the place was awash in red velvet, with that smoky haze covering the soft glow of gaslights. She caught glimpses of overstuffed couches, an upright piano, a large fireplace, potted palms and...

And a great deal of exposed flesh. The ladies of Miss Arlotta's establishment seemed to like to lie around, well, naked. Or more naked than anything she'd ever seen.

As her gaze swept the parlor, Rose saw corsets and filmy wraps, petticoats and stockings, and acres of skin. She'd never seen so many voluptuous curves. Glancing down at her own modest bosom under her brown wool traveling suit, she wondered whether she was cut out to be a lady of the evening after all.

How exotic they looked, draped over low-slung settees and chairs, a few intently playing faro or poker around the card tables, one tapping out a tune on the piano and trilling along, something that culminated in an enthusiastic "Oooh la la!" every other line. Another, a tall, handsome woman with dark red hair, puffed away on a small cigar as she adjusted the pearl-handled revolver stuck in the garter strapped to her thigh.

A gun? An exposed thigh? Scandalous. And yet it was the most thrilling thing Rose had ever seen. They seemed so free, so decadent, so…lush. Who knew sin could look this exciting on an otherwise dull Sunday afternoon in a no-account mining town?

"Miss?" the doorman prompted, tugging at her sleeve. "Wasn't you wanting to see Miss Arlotta?"

"Why, yes, I…" As his broad back disappeared down a hall to the left, Rose had no choice but to follow. She consoled herself that she could come back to the parlor and the gambling tables soon enough, once she was a full-fledged soiled dove like the rest of them. She had some lingerie in her luggage, although nothing like what they were wearing. But maybe if she stripped down to her favorite French chemise, the one with the tiny rosebuds embroidered around the neckline, with her brocade corset and her laciest knickers…

Rose started to feel warm and wicked just thinking about strolling around in her drawers. Maybe she could get one of those guns to stick in her garter, to dramatically reveal at opportune moments.

But she hadn't counted on how intimidating Miss Arlotta would be. Quite the dragon in her lair, the madam of this establishment stood behind a large mahogany desk, staring at Rose with hard, shrewd eyes. She had pale, not-quite-yellow hair, the color of lemonade in the summer sun, coiled in high, stiff ringlets across the top of her head. A fake color *and* fake hair, if Rose had to guess. Miss Arlotta's dress was even more shocking, with a red satin bodice dipping low in the front and folds of the same scarlet fabric pulled back at her ample hips to reveal a shocking black lace underskirt. But that was an evening dress, and all wrong for this time of day. Not to mention the fact that she appeared to be sporting a bustle back there, when everyone knew bustles had been out since 1890.

Miss Arlotta sent Rose a shrewd glance. "Never seen a tart with spectacles before."

She'd forgotten she was wearing her glasses. Hastily Rose removed them and stuck them in her pocket.

"How old are you?"

"Twenty-one." She told the truth, not sure whether it was better to be older or younger for the purposes of a house of ill repute.

"You a virgin?" the madam asked boldly.

Rose gulped. "Well, as a matter of fact, no."

"Didn't think so. That's good. I run my place on the level, you see. Nobody too young, nobody too innocent, and nobody lying about neither," she said in a throaty, no-nonsense tone as she came out from behind the desk, circling around Rose, eyeing her up and down and back again. "Five to one, I already got your number."

"Five to one? What does that mean?" she asked eagerly.

Miss Arlotta ignored the interruption. "Your clothes tell me you come from money. My wager is, some handsome gent seduced you hopin' to get his hands on your daddy's cash. So Daddy figured out what was goin' on and kicked you to the curb. You ran to your beau, but he backed away fast without Daddy's money to sweeten the pot. So now you're thinking you might like to ply your trade as a doxy to get back at both your no-good man and your pa. Am I right?"

It was disappointing to be read so easily. Not to mention being called a *doxy* when there were so many other more romantic choices. Odalisque, *fille de joie*... Much more interesting than *doxy*. "I guess it's a tale you've heard before."

"I've heard most all of 'em." Miss Arlotta poured herself a shot of whiskey from a bottle on the sideboard. "A little skinny, aren't you?"

"With different clothing I think my curves might do," Rose said quickly, doing her best to hold her head high and slant her chest forward at the same time she pushed back her derriere.

That got a smile out of the boss. "I suppose you're old enough to know your own mind," she declared. "And pretty enough to pull in some male admirers. I also think you got too much starch in your drawers and too much book-learnin' for the likes of us, but if you want to try, we'll give you a chance."

"Really?"

"Pete," she barked out, "take the lady's bag to the empty maid's room on the third floor." Turning back, she added, "It ain't much, but we'll move you some-place better if you last any time at all."

Pete, the large man who'd shown her in, opened the door behind her, still carrying her bag. Rose swallowed. She hadn't expected things to move quite so quickly. "When do I, um, begin?" she asked, trying to keep the tremble from her voice. "Will you give me any sort of training?"

Miss Arlotta arched one pale eyebrow. "I figgered you knew what to do when you walked into a bordello and asked for work. You sayin' you need instruction?"

"Well, maybe a little..."

The madam laughed out loud. "You're never going to last at this game. You're the greenest greenhorn I ever did see. I'll put my money down that you'll be heading for the hills at, oh, just about one minute after noon tomorrow."

"I'm not as innocent as you think," Rose replied, edging toward the door. But curiosity pushed her to turn back. "Why did you pick that exact time? Why one minute after noon?"

Miss Arlotta shook her head, not dislodging her tight curls one iota. "Because today is Sunday, we don't do any business here, on account of it being the Lord's day."

Oh, yes. The Sunday picnic the small boy had mentioned. Apparently, even shady ladies took a day of rest.

"So," her new boss continued, "I figure you'll last through tonight. But come start of business tomorrow, round about noon, when you face off with an actual, real-live man taking off his actual, real-live pants..."

Rose tried not to blush, faint or otherwise embarrass herself as Miss Arlotta finished up with, "Then, at just about one minute after twelve, I reckon you'll run screaming for the door."

"You know, I have seen a man without his trousers," she said quickly, trying hard not to let her voice tremble.

A man, to be precise. *One*. But thank goodness she had tonight to gather her wits before she saw another one. And then, on Monday, she would come face-to-face with her new profession as a shameless hussy.

"Right now, you might want to find something else to wear. A lot less, for starters." Her employer puffed up a little when she added, "I hired a photographer to come by this evening to make a tintype of all of my girls, something pretty for the parlor, to help gents make a choice."

Would anyone choose her? Was her lingerie scandalous enough?

Rose had never been in this kind of competition before.

"Oh, and what name should we call you?" the older woman asked. "We like our girls to go by something a little more fancy here."

A new name? It made her feel mysterious and exciting, to have a *nom de plume*. Or *nom de harlot*, anyway.

"Name?" Miss Arlotta prompted.

"Let's see..."

Trying to think of a pseudonym, Rose suddenly remembered her favorite dime novel, stowed safely in her suitcase with her other most-prized possessions. *Little Rosebud's Lovers* by Miss Laura Jean Libbey. The heroine of the book had also found herself ruined and abandoned. Of course, she'd come to a terrible end, it being fiction, but still... It was perfect.

"Rosebud," she announced with a smile. "You can call me Rosebud."

"That'll do fine. Welcome to my establishment, Rosebud," the boss lady said with a wink. She picked up her shot glass and tossed back the whiskey. "I'll lay you ten to one you'll be out of here before you get a chance to try out your new name. But maybe you will surprise me."

"I'll be here longer than that, I assure you, Miss Arlotta."

"I guess we'll see, won't we?"

Rose lifted her chin. How hard could it be?

A Monday in July
Maiden Falls, Colorado, 2004

"ROSEBUD? Get up here! We got a live one for you!"

Secure in her hidey-hole tucked under the eaves in the attic, Rosebud concentrated on page 203 of *East of Eden*, pretending she had not heard the ghostly call to arms from Miss Arlotta. She had no desire for an assignment, no matter how "live" it was.

"Troubled couple on the road to bedroom bliss, blah, blah, blah," she muttered. It wasn't her fault that the entire group of scarlet women—once so good at helping men stray—had been roped into service as celestial matchmakers for honeymooners too pathetic to know how to pleasure each other.

After all, she hadn't even spent one day as a soiled dove herself. What did she know about pleasure? On her very first night in Miss Arlotta's establishment, just hours after choosing her *nom de harlot*, she had passed into the afterlife with all the rest of them. Nobody knew exactly what happened, although the *Maiden Falls Gazette* had claimed it was due to a gas leak, offering the smug opinion that it was exactly what Miss Arlotta deserved for having airs above her station and making her tawdry social club the first place in Colorado outside Denver with gaslights. Whatever the cause, every girl in the place, plus Miss Arlotta and the beau who'd been visiting her that Sunday night, had ended up as dead as cold mackerel, most still tucked into their beds.

As for Rosebud... She'd just been caught in the wrong place at the absolute wrong time.

Of course, that argument had not swayed anyone in this household. Judge Hangen, Miss Arlotta's gentleman friend, had shot back that he, too, had been erroneously stuck in Bordello Purgatory by virtue of bad timing, that there was no leniency provision for girls who hadn't technically had the opportunity for harlotry, and Rosebud was going to have to play by the same rules as the rest of them. Case closed.

"It's completely unfair!" she said angrily, slapping down her book, unable to concentrate when she thought about the terrible injustice of her predicament.

She'd only managed to make it through the 109 years since all their mortal lives had ended by keeping her nose firmly stuck in her books. She'd started with *Little Rosebud's Lovers* and *Lady Audley's Secret*, which she'd been in the process of unpacking from her valise when she passed over the threshold into the spirit world on that fateful night. But she'd tired of reading and rereading just those two, so she'd quickly learned to steal (or borrow, as she preferred to call it) interesting items from visitors to the Inn at Maiden Falls.

In the first dark years, she'd had to depend upon newspapers and the occasional dime novel left by the workmen and ruffians who'd wandered through. Thank goodness the old brothel had been turned into a gaming house, a speakeasy, a saloon, then completely restored and polished up into a high-class honeymoon hotel. The clientele and the reading material had picked up nicely.

Years ago, someone had discarded *Lady Chatterley's Lover*, which she quite adored. The naughty bits in that one always cheered her up. Not to mention *East of Eden*, and more recently several issues of *Entertainment Weekly* and a DVD called *Buffy the Vampire Slayer* that was really quite extraordinary. Things had become so much more interesting since her day!

She used to have to sneak into empty guest rooms to use the televisions, but then one day she'd tripped over something in the Inn's business office called a computer. Which was connected to another bizarre concept called the Internet. Which opened up a whole new world of possibilities for a smart girl who found the modern world quite fascinating.

No one seemed bothered by the assortment of packages from strange and exotic merchants that arrived at the Inn at Maiden Falls. They always thought the mysterious electronic devices, movies, books and music had been ordered by the proper people at the Inn. Rosebud was very careful to fill out all the proper paperwork and purchase orders on the Accounting Department's computers. It wasn't stealing if she charged it to the Inn. Exactly.

"Well, I do bargain shop. And I return every book and movie that isn't an absolute necessity, right back into the Inn's library," Rosebud noted as she slipped *East of Eden* onto her bookshelf next to *Everything You Always Wanted to Know About Sex But Were Afraid to*

Ask. "Besides, how else was a girl supposed to keep herself entertained for 109 years?"

"Rosebud?" Miss Arlotta's voice barked. "Get your pretty behind up here! Where are you, anyway?"

She sounded perturbed, and Rosebud knew she was going to have to show up just so the boss didn't figure out how it was possible for her to be missing and unaccounted for. As far as Rosebud knew, no one else had figured out how to master the fine art of slipping under Miss A's radar, which was just one of her singular skills.

"As long as I have to be a ghost, I may as well be good at it," Rosebud said tartly to no one in particular. Louder, letting her voice float over to the main part of the attic, she called, "Coming, Miss Arlotta."

"Well, I hope so! Where ya been, girl?" the madam demanded.

"Just resting," Rosebud returned coolly as she slid her vaguely corporeal form into place in front of the desk.

"Like you got anything to rest from. Get a move on. I got a job for you."

Although she was only partially visible at the moment, preferring to affect a sort of shimmery, translucent look so as not to let on how very good at materializing she'd become, Rosebud offered an innocent look. "Me? I thought I was on suspension. Isn't there anyone else you'd rather give it to?"

"The place is hoppin' all summer. We need every hand on deck."

"Hand? On deck?" Rosebud echoed doubtfully.

"Every girl has to pull her weight, darlin'. So far, you

have one notch in the Bedpost Book. Total. One notch," Miss Arlotta said grimly. "We been here 109 years and you got a sum total of eighteen black marks, no gold stars, and one lousy notch. And I'm still not convinced that one wasn't just dumb luck."

Rosebud said nothing. As a matter of fact, her one notch in the Bedpost Book, for successfully helping a guest couple turn up the heat on their honeymoon, had been an accident. Annoyed with a young woman who simply would not shut up, Rosebud had filled up the bathtub and knocked her into it. She figured the little twit had to be quiet if she was under water. How was she supposed to guess that the silly groom would find his dripping wet bride particularly erotic?

"Let's just say you aren't exactly hotfootin' it on the road to that Big Picnic in the Sky," the boss went on. "After the way you spun the bed around on the last couple I gave you, I ought to leave you on permanent suspension. Scared the living daylights out of 'em and sprained the groom's leg when he tried to jump out."

"I really deserve suspension," Rosebud agreed, batting her eyelashes and trying to look contrite. The truth was, she liked being suspended. As long as it lasted, she was free to read and watch movies to her heart's content. And she was expecting the six-hour DVD of *Pride and Prejudice* to arrive at the front desk any day. Surely her suspension could last long enough to get through *Pride and Prejudice*.

"If you don't ever get your ten notches in the Bedpost Book, me and the judge are stuck here like two pigs in tar, right along with you," Miss Arlotta explained impatiently. "You know that. This ain't just for you. Me and the judge can only move on after all you girls are gone."

"Yes, but—"

"No buts. Everybody knows you're not carrying your load. That crazy Flo, who hasn't been happy a day since 1895 on account of her corset problems, has got more notches than you. You're a smart girl, Rosebud. I'm giving you a job that ought to be a walk in the park."

Bad choice of phrase, considering the goal they were all trying to reach was the Big Picnic, where they looked forward to walking in the park throughout eternity. Rosebud wasn't so sure about it, however. She wanted to be certain there was a wide-screen TV and a stack of DVDs and books waiting or she didn't really want to go.

The madam interrupted her thoughts, snapping, "You better make this one work, Rosebud, or I don't know what I'm gonna do with you. Get off your fanny and go see the bride. Name of Vanessa Westicott. She's rich and spoiled, just like you used to be, so she ought to be a kindred spirit."

Rosebud chewed her lip. Funny how she could still feel pain when she bit down, considering the lip wasn't technically there. "I don't suppose there's any way to get out of this?"

"Nope. Get to it. She's in the lobby, looking over the place right now. While she gets showed around, you can give her the once-over and think up a plan." Miss Arlotta narrowed her eyes. "With all those books you read, you ought to be real good at that."

"MAYBE I CAN GET this over with and get my notch in the Bedpost Book lickety split, just in time for my DVDs to arrive," Rosebud mused as she wafted down to the lobby.

She saw a group of the other ghostly girls lounging around in what had once been their front parlor, as transparent and indistinct as their lingerie, but she didn't join them. The only two she'd really liked among the bunch—sweet Sunshine and cantankerous, shoot-from-the-hip Belle—the one who'd been smoking the cigar in the parlor on the day Rosebud arrived—had already passed over the threshold into the Great Beyond. And the others were so dreary.

She hadn't realized, when she'd signed on for this job all those years ago, that hookers were not, as a rule, incredibly bright. Flo and her whining about her too-tight corset (stuck that way until someone figured out how to loosen her ghostly corset strings) got old very quickly, while Mimi and her fake French accent and Desdemoaner, nicknamed for all the caterwauling she used to do while in the throes of passion, were downright annoying. And then there was the Countess.

"Countess, my eye," Rosebud griped, just thinking about it. "I have more class in my little finger than that chippy has in her entire body."

Flo, Des, the Countess, even lush and lovely Lavender... All they ever talked about was *men*. They seemed to enjoy helping hapless couples jump the hurdle into marital bliss, but they also whined constantly about how much they wished they could get in a few licks with the grooms they were assigned. Which was, of course, against the rules.

The rule itself didn't bother Rosebud nearly as much as all the complaining about it. She didn't have much sympathy for the hapless honeymooners they were supposed to be helping, but she wasn't going to pine over how sad it was she didn't get to engage in spectral sex with their grooms, either.

But for the moment... For the moment, she was going to have to see about this Vanessa person and make some move to help the poor, pathetic girl with her honeymoon, at least enough to earn another notch in Miss A's infernal Bedpost Book and keep the boss off her back for a while. Even Rosebud, the least successful ghostly good-time girl in the place, knew very well that Miss Arlotta and the Judge wielded mighty powers. Nobody was sure where their authority came from or exactly what they were capable of, but they all knew not to mess with Miss A.

But where was the sexually inept bride-to-be? Rosebud glanced around the check-in desk, but she didn't see her target. She saw two front desk clerks, a bellman and several couples who were clearly honeymooners. One coosome twosome was canoodling on a velvet settee behind a potted palm, while another groom had his bride in his lap while he fed her little tidbits of crackers and cheese from the buffet set up for the cocktail hour. Everybody else was more of the same. Lovey-dovey, gooey-schmooey. Rosebud rolled her eyes. Clearly they didn't need help. Other than that...

The only other person in the lobby at the moment was a man by himself. *Oooh. Yummy.* Dark suit, dark hair, tall, broad-shouldered, and quite delicious to look at from the back side.

She squinted at him, wishing she knew how to get new spectacles over the Internet. The ones she'd passed over with were the best 1895 had to offer, but they left the modern world a bit too fuzzy.

Especially when there was something this good to look at.

She swooshed past the potted palm couple, making the woman shiver and cuddle closer to her husband. Rosebud ignored them, intent on getting a better look at the intriguing man by the window. But he was still facing the other way, pulling back one of the heavy drapes to gaze out the front window of the Inn.

"Turn around," she whispered, vainly attempting to plant thoughts in his head. If only Belle were still here. She was so good at that.

Unfortunately Rosebud didn't share Belle's skills. Manipulating gadgets and electronics, remembering and recreating music she'd heard only once, a knack for remaining unnoticed by Miss Arlotta's all-seeing eyes, and the ability to make herself so 3-D it would knock your socks off.... Those were her talents. Not that they did her a particle of good at the moment.

Rosebud cocked her head to one side, trying to figure out why she was so intrigued by this man. Yes, she liked the looks of him, but it was more than that.

She felt oddly drawn to him. It was the strangest thing. She just had to know who he was, what he was doing there, and especially what he looked like. *All* of him, dadblast it!

"First time for everything," she murmured. Out of all the men who'd wandered through the Inn over the years, this was the first one who'd made her feel this curious warmth, this shiver of anticipation and... And what seemed to be lust.

"It's not lust," she said under her breath. She wasn't like the other girls with their constant urge to merge. "Just curiosity."

Maybe if she blew on his neck. Or in his ear. Or flickered the lights in the parlor. How about a little jolt of electricity transmitted through a pinch to his adorable derriere? If she gave him a tiny shock, surely he would have to turn to face her.

She checked behind her to see if any of the other girls had noticed him (or her fascination with him) but they seemed to be intent on some silly bickering over a card game in the far corner. She was safe for the moment, if she could just get him to turn around...

"You're supposed to be looking for a woman." Miss Arlotta's aggravated tone rang in Rosebud's ear, making her jump. "Tell me, does that gent look like a woman?"

"Not even a little," Rosebud responded without thinking.

"The gal you're looking for is in the ballroom," the boss interrupted. "She's about decided she doesn't want her wedding here. If she walks, your goose is good and cooked. So get a move on."

Much as she hated to tear herself away from the mysterious man at the window, Rosebud knew she had no choice but to leave him behind. Drat.

"Miss A told me my bride was in the lobby," she complained out loud, reluctantly floating away from the man at the window. "How was I supposed to know she'd be in the ballroom?"

"Did you hear that? I could swear I heard a female voice talking about the ballroom, right in my ear," the woman with the crackers whispered as Rosebud swooped past. "And I can feel a chill."

"They say this place has ghosts," her husband told her, holding her close.

Real wizards, those two. But Rosebud had forgotten herself for a moment. Apparently her long suspension had made her people skills rusty. *Inaudible, you ninny,* she told herself. *Neither seen nor heard.* She managed to keep her mouth shut as she flashed into the ballroom to catch up with her new assignment.

And there she was. The bride du jour.

"I don't like the looks of her at all," Rosebud remarked as she sailed up to take a position behind the main chandelier. "She looks like the Countess, doesn't she? And every bit as snooty."

Vanessa Westicott looked sharp, in every sense of the word. Her hair, as dark as Rosebud's own, was pulled back into a severe knot at the back of her neck. From the pained expression on her face, the knot was too tight. She was pretty, very thin, and dressed in a snappy little black outfit with a skirt that Rosebud found scandalously short. And the woman was wearing high-heeled, pointy black boots that were not going to be comfortable as she toured the Inn.

Right now she was peering up at the chandelier Rosebud was swinging from, pinching her mouth together and making her unhappiness quite clear to one of the hotel's wedding coordinators, a sweet young woman named Beth, who was giving her the grand tour.

"Wicked Witch of the West," Rosebud whispered, swirling around the woman for a closer look. She'd watched *The Wizard of Oz* a few weeks ago, so the image was fresh in her mind. "All she needs is a green face."

"What did you say?" Vanessa turned on her guide. "Green plates? Why in the world would I want that?"

"I didn't say anything about green plates."

"Well, I don't like this ballroom, no matter what color scheme we use on the table settings," Vanessa snapped. "The lighting is terrible."

"These chandeliers are reproductions of what was here in 1895, without the gas, of course," Beth said quickly.

But Vanessa had moved on, tapping her pointy foot on the parquet floor. "What kind of wood is this? I don't like it. I prefer walnut."

As if she would recognize walnut if she fell over it. Rosebud rolled her ghostly eyes. Princess Vanessa was a pain. A royal pain.

It went on that way as the tour continued, with Beth leading Vanessa on to the next space, a lovely, intimate private dining room recommended for the rehearsal dinner, and then up to the guest rooms. But the bride-to-be's list of demands just kept getting longer, and she wanted it all at rock-bottom prices.

Beluga caviar. Cristal champagne. Special lace tablecloths from Belgium. Special caterer. Special masseuse. And on and on, down to her insistence on the Inn's best honeymoon suite, although all the linens were going to have to be changed. She required Egyptian cotton with 800-thread counts, of course.

"This suite is the only thing you've got that's even slightly acceptable for my honeymoon," she sniffed, running a finger over the edge of a mahogany side table.

Hrmph. Rosebud might not have been the happiest hooker on the premises, but after 109 years, she had a certain loyalty to the place. Besides, she'd once lived in the lap of Denver society—during an era far more elegant than this one—and she knew there was nothing wrong with the Inn at Maiden Falls or its rooms or its chef or its linens or anything else.

And certainly not the gorgeous suite they were standing in, the one they called the Lady Godiva Suite, which reminded Rosebud of the inside of a candy box with its deep reds and pinks and chocolaty browns. Like the rest of the Inn, it was full of antiques and featured a beautiful, sensual pre-Raphaelite painting, one of the odalisques, over the fireplace in its sitting room. Right now, there were fresh flowers, a display of fine chocolates and a bottle of excellent champagne on ice, all awaiting tonight's lucky guests.

Rosebud adored this room. She hoped Beth told Princess Vanessa to zip her narrow scarlet lips very soon, or she might just have to shove her out the window of the Lady Godiva Suite.

"But if she dies on the premises, with my luck she'll be stuck here with the rest of us into eternity," she grumbled.

The wedding coordinator was more diplomatic. "I can look into some of your other requests, but I can't promise you this suite," Beth said gently, referring back to her notes. "The Inn is insanely popular, and your dates are awfully soon. Are you at all flexible about, say, midweek? We may even be booked for those, but that's your best shot."

"You do know who my fiancé is, don't you?" Vanessa asked, raising one dark sliver of an eyebrow.

Rosebud was curious about that herself. Who would willingly hitch themselves to Vanessa's wagon?

Beth blinked. "I'm aware that his uncle is one of our owners, yes. To be honest, that's why we're trying to accommodate you. Normally you'd have to book at least a year ahead. If not two. Because your fiancé's uncle made a special request, we will do everything we can. But we can't squeeze out someone who's already reserved the space. I'm sure you understand."

"I'm not sure I want to get married here, anyway," the bride said with a frown. "Retro-Victorian kitsch is *so* yesterday. The whole place just reeks of Nothing Special to me."

"Oh, it's very special." As Beth led her charge into the hallway, Rosebud ignored the locked door and lazily passed through the thick wood to join them. "We don't really advertise it, but the Inn has a unique reputation."

The bride-to-be looked a bit more interested. "I heard that Daphne Remington got married here, but I never thought she was all that. What level are you talking? Jennifer and Brad? Gwyneth and Chris? Or *real* royalty?"

"Although our clientele includes some very fine names, it's not about that," Beth said quickly. "It's more the atmosphere."

Vanessa lifted her narrow shoulders in a shrug. "I'm not feeling any atmosphere."

"Well, you see..."

"Yes? What?"

"Around the turn of the century, it was a bordello," the wedding coordinator confided. "A fancy bordello. There's this theory that the women who worked here are still here, sort of, um, hanging around the rafters, if you get my drift."

"Like, ghosts?" There was that eyebrow again. "Ghosts of old *hookers?* Is that what you're saying?"

"In so many words, yes." Beth smiled as they neared the elevator. "Let's just say that everyone seems to have a really good time when they stay here, and we think it may be because there are some lusty spirits giving them a little boost. I've seen and heard some things—"

"I don't believe in ghosts," Vanessa said flatly. "It all sounds ridiculous to me. And obscene. Ghost *hookers.* Yechhh."

Obscene? Rosebud took issue with that. She had never done anything obscene in her entire life, and none of the others, not even the Countess, fell to that level. What was wrong with helping honeymooners have more fun?

"Just between you and me," the bride-to-be went on, "I'm only considering it because of the family connection. But I don't know..."

"We have a lot of happy brides and grooms," Beth put in.

"Yes, but we're no ordinary bride and groom. We're very choosy."

Which did not come as a surprise to Rosebud.

"Well, not every property is right for every couple," the wedding planner noted. "Maybe you'd be happier choosing a different location."

Good for you, Beth! Give her the boot! But Vanessa didn't seem to have noticed the message behind Beth's tactfully phrased words.

Frowning, the bride-to-be muttered, "Ned seems to think this place is our only option with so little time to plan."

Ned. So that was the name of the poor bridegroom shackled to the Wicked Witch.

"If time is the problem, maybe you should consider pushing back the date," Beth said helpfully. "A year, even two, would open things up. You might even want to pick your date based on when you can get your first choice of location."

"Wait another year? Not a chance," Vanessa declared. "I've been waiting for Ned to propose for two years. I know him. If I don't pounce, he'll back out. So I'm pouncing. If that means getting married in this dump, so be it."

Dump? As the elevator arrived, Rosebud briefly contemplated letting Vanessa get stuck in it for a good, long time. But she wasn't that good with elevators, plus that would trap Beth, too, and that hardly seemed fair.

Perhaps a small slip and fall... But there were no raw materials hanging around in the hallway to create any interesting tricks, so she had to let it go. For now.

"Let's go down to my office and look at what exactly we have available in August," Beth said soothingly as she pulled back the brass door to usher Vanessa into the elevator. "Once everything is set, I know you'll love having your wedding here at the Inn."

As those two rode the elevator down, Rosebud took her own route, sliding smoothly through the floors and showing up ahead of them at the sales office. As she dawdled by the door to Beth's office, she mused, "What to do? What to do?"

There were so many dirty tricks it would be fun to pull on Vanessa when she came back for her wedding in August. "Floods and blizzards and all that good stuff were really more Sunshine's thing, but I might be able to screw up a little plumbing and generate a nice-size flood."

"Don't even think it," Miss Arlotta's voice admonished her sternly. "Remember the Bedpost Book, with all those black marks and no gold stars and only that one little notch? If you do anything to monkey with this bride's happy honeymoon, you are going to be one sorry sister. Count on it."

"Yes, but she's extremely unpleasant," Rosebud argued. "It shouldn't be my job to sentence some poor man to a life sentence with *that*. She'll eat him alive before their first anniversary."

Miss Arlotta's head popped up in front of her, fully visible. Just her head. This was not only highly unusual, but it was downright frightening!

"We don't get to pick 'em. We just have to make 'em happy. Shape up, Rosebud," she barked. "You're skating on thin ice."

At that, the head popped out of sight, just before Beth and the bride turned the corner and headed that way. Trying to forget the disturbing image of Miss A's disembodied head hanging in the air, Rosebud focused on the task at hand. She was going to have to swallow her dislike and make this work, because the boss had made it crystal clear she didn't have any other choice. And even Rosebud was afraid of Miss Arlotta's powers, murky as they were.

"How hard can it be?" she asked. "I'll make sure stupid Vanessa enjoys a torrid honeymoon, and then..."

But wait a second. Vanessa and Beth weren't alone. There was a man with them. A handsome man. Rosebud stared. Dark hair, dark suit. The man from the window. And yet...

If she'd had a jaw at that moment, it would've dropped to the floor. *She knew him.*

"Ned, I'm so glad you decided to join us." Vanessa swiped her thumb across his cheek to remove a smear of red lipstick. "Now that you're here, darling, you can tell me all the reasons you like this place, and maybe I can be persuaded to like it, too."

Rosebud was absolutely thunderstruck. Miss Arlotta's warning echoed in her mind. *You're skating on thin ice...*

She didn't care if she was skating on icebergs. She knew him! The clothes and the cut of his hair might be different, but his eyes and his smile and the way he carried himself, exuding confidence and charm, were exactly the same, the same as Edmund Mulgrew, the man who had turned her from an innocent girl into a fallen maiden so long ago.

Edmund?

For the first time in 109 years, Rosebud felt her heart go pitter-patter.

2

A Tuesday in August
Maiden Falls, Colorado, 2004

ROSEBUD WAS A BUNDLE of nerves. Tonight. Ned was coming back to the hotel tonight. He was due to check in at about nine o'clock tonight according to the itinerary she'd filched from Beth's desk. If she just waited a few more hours, she'd get to see him again. If she didn't expire from anticipation first.

It didn't help that the Inn was an absolute zoo and had been for weeks, with too many brides and grooms and Miss Arlotta watching her like a hawk. Here she was again, ready with a lecture.

"Your bride's comin' in any minute," the madam said grimly, one hand on her wide hip. "Her and the groom's got a fancy dinner tomorrow, stag parties the next night, wedding Friday night. They're leaving the morning after the wedding, so you'll have to get the fire blazing now." She eyed Rosebud suspiciously. "You ready?"

"Yes, ma'am."

She tried to keep her physical image as indistinct as possible so Miss Arlotta couldn't read her expression. She'd been so stunned when she first saw Ned that she hadn't been careful, giving away too much. Her boss had gotten the idea pretty quickly that something was weird about this one.

"So you got all your plans locked and loaded for the Westicott gal and her intended? What's his name again?"

"Ned," Rosebud replied, trying to sound nonchalant. "Ned Mulgrew." She'd verified that much from the files in the Sales office.

Mulgrew. What were the odds? It had never occurred to her to use her laptop to find out whatever happened to the people she'd once known, maybe because she'd acquired the thing so long after she left them all behind. It was a different world now. Who knew there would be Mulgrews in it?

But once she'd spotted Ned in the lobby, she had to know. Was there a connection? Was her memory playing tricks on her? Could it be?

It could. Her quick search on the Internet had found very little on Edmund, but he must've married into the money he'd wanted so badly back then. Or perhaps he'd stolen it. However he'd managed to climb the ladder of success, his children's children had become the cream of Denver society. Including his great-grandson Ned Mulgrew, age thirty, a lawyer with a top Denver firm, engaged to the equally wealthy Vanessa Westicott. Rosebud didn't understand a thing about Ned's job—something about corporate mergers and acquisitions—but his face seemed to appear in the newspaper a lot. And it was a very nice face.

A lot nicer than his great-grandfather's, she'd decided. Ned seemed to have a sincerity about his smile that Edmund had lacked. And maybe a tinge of sadness in his beautiful blue eyes. Of course, it was hard to tell without seeing him close up...

"What's his problem? Too cold? Too hard? Not into the ladies?" Miss Arlotta interrogated. "Why did he and his intended land in our laps for a quick fix?"

"Well, I don't know. I mean, I, um, only saw him that once. The day they came to look at the hotel," Rosebud said hastily. "But he looked, well, *fine*. Extra fine." With a little more enthusiasm than she'd intended, she added, "I don't think there's anything wrong with Ned."

"Uh-huh," her boss said with an edge of sarcasm. "So I gather you liked what you saw?"

She barely stopped herself from gushing, *Oh, yesssss.* Instead she murmured, "I don't think he's the problem."

"So she is?"

"Vanessa?" Rosebud couldn't keep the scorn from her voice. "She's a piece of work, that one."

She had now seen enough of Vanessa Westicott to last a lifetime. She might've forgiven the princess her tantrums and hissy fits if she'd only brought Ned back to the hotel with her. Rosebud had been on pins and needles hoping he'd come back. But no. Every visit since that first one Vanessa had made by herself.

And every time, she'd had new demands, new complaints, until everyone in the hotel was sick of her. If it weren't for the fact that Ned Mulgrew's uncle was one of the owners, Vanessa and her diva antics would've been tossed out onto the street long ago.

"I can tell you that she's the one who wants to get married, and she's in a hurry so he won't change his mind." Rosebud frowned. "What I don't know is why he wanted to marry that ice princess in the first place."

"If all the brides and grooms were perfect, there'd be no need for us, would there?" Miss Arlotta asked darkly. "So you need to put a little giddy-up in her gallop. Shouldn't be too hard if the boy is as fine as all that."

Rosebud had no idea what that meant but it sounded unpleasant. "Giddy-up in her gallop. Right. I'm on it."

"What's your plan?"

"Oh." She blinked. "Well, I'm kind of playing it by ear."

"You've had a month to plan, Rosebud," Miss Arlotta said ominously. "Don't let me down. Make it work. Stick with the bride if she's the problem. Feed her some oysters and a lot of wine, shove her right into his bed and turn up the heat. Tonight. Time's a-wastin'."

Rosebud winced. Ned in bed with Vanessa? That was an image she didn't need infecting her brain. "I'll do my best, but..."

"But what?"

But I don't want him with her! I just found him, and I only got to see him once, and I don't think it's at all fair that I should have to help some other woman have him.

And the idea of supervising or improving their erotic activities? *Eeeeuw!*

"What?" Miss Arlotta asked again, more forcefully this time. "What's the holdup?"

"Nothing," Rosebud said quickly. "I'll do my best."

Her best *what* she left unspecified. She would worry

about the pesky problem of how to help Ned and Vanessa in bed later. As for right now…

Rosebud felt excitement sizzle through her veins. *Ned is coming. Tonight.* She glanced at the cuckoo clock over Miss Arlotta's desk. Five-fifteen. Less than four hours, and Ned would be here.

She had been waiting for this moment ever since she'd laid eyes on him. Ned. The spitting image of her beloved, that rascal Edmund.

Once he was here, she didn't know whether she should kick him or kiss him. She had spent the better part of a month debating exactly that. Which was why she hadn't bothered to come up with a plan for Vanessa.

She was much more interested in Ned. Who was he? Would he be anything like his great-grandfather? And what was he doing engaged to a witch like Vanessa?

She itched to find out.

"I don't know why you're still up here. Your bride is already checking in," Miss Arlotta noted, making a shooing motion with one ghostly hand. "Day late and a dollar short before you even start. Rosebud, I swear, you're gonna be the death of me yet."

Rosebud refrained from pointing out that Miss Arlotta was already dead. Jittery with nerves over the idea of seeing Ned later—and having to deal with the odious Vanessa first—she murmured, "I'm going, I'm going."

But as she flashed down to the lobby, she heard Miss Arlotta's unamused voice in her ear. "Don't even think about botchin' this one, Rosebud. I'm keepin' my eye on you."

"Don't worry," she responded sweetly. "I'll be on my best behavior."

"That's what I'm afraid of."

Luckily for Rosebud, the hotel was packed to the gills, so she knew it wouldn't be as easy as all that for Miss A to monitor her, especially when the other girls were providing such good cover with their own assignments. Mimi had been complaining since yesterday about a frightened virgin of a bride who kept locking herself in the bathroom, while Glory wanted everyone to drop everything and check out her groom, because she said he had the smallest equipment she'd ever seen and it was going to be impossible to strike any sparks with that tiny thing to work with. Every time she started to describe her groom and his "Wee Willie Winkie," she dissolved into giggles, which got Desdemoaner going with the honking snort she called a laugh.

That meant there were two ghost harlots rolling around the attic, wheezing with laughter, while Mimi swore in French and stamped her tiny foot and demanded help with her fraidy-cat bride. Not to mention Flo and the usual whines about her constricted corset and the snooty Countess offering unwanted opinions on the side while everybody told her to tend to her own assignment.

With all that, Miss Arlotta had her hands full, and Rosebud felt very comfortable that whatever tricks she got up to with Ned's bride would go unnoticed. Hadn't she always been the smartest Fallen Maiden around? Wasn't it a dead certainty she could outfox

Miss A and the others long enough to have a little fun with...

Uh-oh. Rosebud skittered to a stop at the bottom of the main staircase, a few feet from the front desk.

Ned. Here. Now. Early. She wasn't ready. And yet...

She'd been waiting so long. As she saw Ned standing there in the lobby, Rosebud's mouth went dry and her knees went weak. She felt stirrings in places that hadn't been stirred in 109 years. Wide-eyed, immobile, she clasped both hands hard against the front of her corset, forgetting to breathe for just a second.

He looked amazing. No suit today, just a soft, form-fitting dark sweater and black trousers. He had his hands jammed in his pants pockets, lounging there as if he didn't have a care in the world.

She wanted to touch him. She wanted to press her lips against his. What would it feel like for him if she did? Would one little ghostly kiss trigger anything in him? And how much trouble would she get into if she tried it?

No sign of the other girls or Miss Arlotta. No one to see if she...

Out of nowhere, he turned, narrowing his gaze, staring right at the spot where she lingered by the bottom of the stairs. And then he smiled, white teeth flashing between perfect lips, as if he sensed her presence. As if he *wanted* her presence.

No wonder he was a lawyer. Juries probably melted every time he smiled at them and he never lost a case.

My stars. That was potent stuff. She was a ghost, but still she began to melt from the inside out. Why did he have to be so handsome? The fascinating blue eyes, the enchanting smile, those marvelous lips...

There was a reason she had so easily lost her virtue back in 1895. And she was looking at him.

"Damn you, Ned Mulgrew," she whispered.

"That's weird." He glanced around the bustling lobby. "I could swear somebody just cursed at me. *Damn you, Ned Mulgrew.* That's what I heard. But who would say that?"

"Hmm? What?" Distracted with the check-in process, as well as keeping an eye on the bellman who was carting all fifteen pieces of her matching Louis Vuitton luggage, Vanessa gave her fiancé a glance. "Ned? Did you say something?"

"Nothing important." He leaned over to kiss her on the cheek, moving in closer behind her at the front desk, angling an arm around her in a cozy gesture. Rosebud decided right then and there that kicking him was definitely smarter than kissing him. One minute he was sending come-hither smiles at her across time and space, and the next he was cuddling with the odious Vanessa. Swine.

Maybe he was as greedy and insincere as his ancestor, and he was fleecing Vanessa for every dime of her trust fund. Rosebud hoped so. But it didn't look like it from here. Okay, so his smile didn't quite reach his eyes when he looked at Vanessa. And his features seemed a bit strained. Still...

He was planning to marry the twit, wasn't he?

Rosebud crossed her arms over her chest, debating whether to drop a chandelier on both their heads.

Nah. Miss Arlotta would know who did it. But it was tempting.

She flitted up the stairway to get herself a little farther away from temptation, perching her frilly bloomers on the smooth mahogany banister about halfway up, where she could still eavesdrop. All she needed to do was find out what room they were in, and she could go on ahead, leaving them to their pathetic canoodling at the desk. Then she would ponder a plan of action, and decide whether it would involve pushing them together...

She smiled. Or pulling them apart. That spinning bed thing had worked nicely on the last couple she didn't like.

"You're in the Lady Godiva Suite," the front desk clerk said pleasantly. He pushed a folio across the desk toward Ned for his signature. "That's our best honeymoon suite. I have you down for four nights."

Pulling the paper over her way, Vanessa scrawled her name on it. Then she leaned over and nabbed the brass key out of the clerk's hand. "It's five nights."

"Five? I'll have to check on that. Let me just get another key for Mr. Mulgrew," the clerk murmured, turning back to the wide expanse of cubbyholes where the keys were kept.

"No." Vanessa's lips pressed into a thin scarlet line of displeasure. "He doesn't need a key. The suite is for me."

She wasn't planning to share the honeymoon suite with her fiancé? Now that was interesting. Ned. Lady Godiva Suite. Both dark and delicious. Honestly, how could anyone think about those two items and not want to put them together? Immediately.

"There is a separate reservation for my fiancé," the bride-to-be continued, starting to sound a little testy. "For a separate room."

Well, maybe she was a virgin and she wanted to stay one till her wedding night. Rosebud gave her the once-over. "If she's a virgin, I'm Buffy the Vampire Slayer," Rosebud groused. "So why doesn't she want to share her suite with Ned?"

"Hmmm." The desk clerk consulted his computer. "I don't see anything..."

"Get the manager," Vanessa seethed. "Now."

"Van, it's okay. We'll figure it out."

"You didn't make the arrangements, Ned. I did. I checked and rechecked everything, and that moron of a wedding consultant assured me we were all set. I am stressed out enough with the wedding plans and I need my sleep." She shook her head. "I told you this place wasn't good enough, but you insisted. And now they're making all kinds of mistakes, just like I knew they would."

"We were lucky to get in here," he reminded her. "Uncle Jerry pulled major strings to make it happen. I would've been happy to wait till next year or when-ever we could get whatever palace it was you wanted, but you insisted it had to be now."

"Do not take that tone with me," Vanessa snapped.

Oooh, goodie! Fireworks! Rosebud took a jaunty slide down the banister to get closer. It was beginning to sound as if she wouldn't need to do much work to keep these two apart, what with the separate rooms and all the hostility.

Ned sighed. "Van, we're getting married in three days. Do you really want to argue about this now? Trust me. We'll fix it."

He sounded so calm. Darn it. Fizzling all the fireworks before they got started.

To the desk clerk, Ned said, "Do you have another room you can give me? Anything is fine."

"Well, sir... The Inn is packed, I'm afraid. All I have is a small single room tucked into the back of the third floor."

Rosebud gulped. What? A small room tucked into the back of the third floor? There was only one room at the Inn that fit that description. Her old room. The one Miss Arlotta had sent her to on that Sunday night back in 1895.

The clerk continued. "It's available because it's a single, and frankly..." He grinned. "We don't do a lot of business with singles, if you know what I mean. I think it's a nice room, just small. Sometimes an extra bridesmaid takes it. I don't know if—"

"It'll do," Vanessa interrupted. "He said anything was fine."

As Vanessa took off in the elevator with the bellman and all fifteen pieces of her luggage, bound for the Lady Godiva Suite, Rosebud stayed where she was on the banister, her mind reeling.

How bizarre. How *intimate.* Ned, the instant connection, the instant longing, and now... He would be staying in her old room?

If she didn't know better, she might've thought this

was all kismet or destiny or something. Impetuous, romantic Rose Elizabeth Tate had been a firm believer in those things. But Rosebud the cynical spirit, stuck floating in the rafters for the past 109 years, was not.

With his key in hand, Ned picked up his bag and made straight for the big, ornate staircase that curved around behind the desk. Straight for her. Startled, she toppled sideways, falling off the banister onto the bottom step. Ouch.

"Sir, you're on the third floor. You might want to take the elevator," the clerk called out.

"Nah, I'm good." He smiled again and Rosebud weakened, standing up and edging more toward the middle of the staircase, that much closer to his path. It couldn't hurt to reach out, to touch him ever so slightly, could it? He'd never even feel it.

But when he swept past, when she brushed her invisible fingers gently along the line of his jaw, Rosebud began to tremble. *My stars.* She felt warm and shaky and... That was *intense.* She slammed backward with a thump, hitting the newel-post.

"What the hell?" Ned paused on the stairs. With his hand cupping his jaw, right where she'd touched him, he turned around, glancing up and down the staircase.

"Are you okay, sir?" the desk clerk asked from down below.

"I'm, uh, fine. Just fine. For a minute, I thought..." He dropped his hand. "Nothing." And then he started back up the stairs.

It took her a second or two to collect herself, but then Rosebud made up her mind. Miss Arlotta had ordered her to stick with the bride, but she didn't care. There was no way she was running over to the suite to check on the odious Vanessa, no matter how hard Miss A came down on her later for neglecting her duty.

"I'm sticking with *him*," she whispered, hustling along to catch up.

By the time she got to the small room at the back of the third floor, he had his suitcase open on the bed to unpack. Rosebud hung back by the door, afraid to touch him or get in his way after that scary encounter on the stairs.

Who knew what might happen if their atoms collided? Would she burst into flame?

As she looked around, she realized she hadn't been in this room in quite a while, preferring to spend her time in her hideaway in the attic. But it was a pretty room, especially since they'd renovated it along with the rest of the hotel. Now it had an antique sleigh bed in glossy cherry wood, a matching dresser and mirror and a lovely armoire that held the TV and minibar. Plus Ned. She smiled. Who could ask for anything more?

Busy unpacking, he didn't seem to notice the extra presence in the room. Rosebud flitted around the corner to check out the marble bath and sink and then back into the main room, poking her nose into Ned's toiletries and accoutrements. She told herself she was filing away information for later use, but the truth was, she was greedy for knowledge about Ned.

Ooh, he'd unpacked a tuxedo. Basic black, with a white formal shirt and a small black tie. She could only imagine what Ned would look like in that. A lot like Edmund, probably. She swallowed. She had, of course, seen Edmund in formal evening wear quite a few times, and the sight had been devastatingly handsome. But Ned... Ned was even better.

As he crossed to the phone, leaving a message for someone about picking up his tuxedo to take to the cleaners, she couldn't hold herself back. She slipped over to finger the tucks down the front of his formal shirt, leaning into the closet, inhaling the scent of him that clung to his clothes. She began to pick through the hangers. Button-down shirts, a suit jacket in a smooth wool...

"I'm losing it," he said out loud, taking a step toward the closet. "First I hear my name and there's nobody there, then that weird thing on the stairs, and now my clothes are moving all by themselves."

Ooops. She hadn't realized she'd lifted the sleeve of his suit jacket up to her nose. As unobtrusively as she could manage, Rosebud let it drop back into place. She edged her way around the outside of the room, skirting carefully around Ned to the window next to the bed. Quietly she eased it open, letting in the cool mountain air. On the other side of the room, Ned was fixated on the closet, moving one hanger at a time, staring at his clothes as if he expected them to sprout wings.

Rosebud flailed her arms around, whipping up the lace curtains at the window. Gaining speed, she swooshed around the room a few times like the spirit of the North Wind. She even made a slight howling noise. It was the best she could think of on short notice.

Ned spun around. "Oh. The window's open." He sighed with relief. "Just a stiff breeze. Of course there's a rational explanation."

Of course. As he shut the window and pulled the curtains closed, Rosebud sighed with relief. Trying to stay out of the way and not get into any more trouble, she stretched out on the sleigh bed, careful not to squash the pillow or make an indentation.

It was strangely enjoyable simply watching Ned move around the room. The other girls were always snickering about some fine manly form or other, but she hadn't paid attention in a long, long time. But now that she looked, she had to say, man-watching did make for a good show. The play of muscle under his shirt was very interesting. And the sight of his trousers, stretching against his tight bottom when he bent over to put away his socks... Mmmm...

Shameless, she told herself as she ogled his derriere. And not fair to Ned. *Why, Rose, you're no better than a voyeur.*

He dumped the contents of his pockets on the dresser with a jingle of keys and change. Then there was a snap as he unbuckled his belt, and her breath caught in her throat. Why was he undoing his belt?

Oh, dear. Belt. Off. Tossed aside. And his hands moved to the bottom edge of his sweater, sliding it up an inch or two over his flat stomach. At the first glimpse of bronzed flesh, Rosebud's eyes widened. What was he doing? He wasn't going to undress, was he?

Why, yes he was. Rosebud went very still as he peeled off his shirt and tossed it toward the bed. Right on top of her. She didn't move, but she did finger the fine silk knit where it slid sensuously over her hip. And she hungrily drank in the sight of him, naked to the waist.

She had forgotten how gorgeous a man could be. Ned's skin gleamed, tanned and smooth in the golden light from the antique lamp on the dresser, and her eyes trailed over his hard chest and torso, ridged with muscle. There was a fine line of dark hair trailing between his ribs, disappearing into his pants. Her mouth watered. Did men look this delectable back in her day?

Ned stopped. His gaze skimmed right over her where she lay on the bed, and he frowned. "Why is there a bump under that shirt?"

Bump? A bump like her? What should she do? Slip out from under the shirt while he was watching, making it clear the unseen lump had moved away and something spooky was going on in his room? Or stay where she was, even if he advanced on her and felt under the shirt? His hand would go right through her while she was invisible. At least she thought it would.

Her heart beat faster, and she couldn't think. Did she want him to touch her, to connect his protoplasm to her ectoplasm, to shock them both down to their toes, even if it meant some irreversible explosion of particles and electricity?

Oh, yes. Right now, after watching him undress, she was totally willing to risk it.

Foolish, foolish girl to get herself in this position. She felt her body suffuse with warmth under his intense gaze, and she had the terrible suspicion that a wash of hot color would show up there on his bed, like a reclining girl-shaped pool of pink. She glanced down but didn't see anything. She'd never blushed before when she was invisible. How did she know what might happen?

Just when she thought she might pop from the strain, Ned's phone rang. He jumped, she jumped, and his shirt slid off her hip at the exact moment he turned toward the phone. Saved by the bell. Rosebud was off his bed and safely huddled on top of the armoire, hiding up next to the ceiling, before he'd even answered it.

"Hello," he said impatiently. But then his voice changed to a much warmer tone. "Hi, Uncle Jerry. Thanks so much for setting everything up. We really appreciate you making it happen. Your hotel is wonderful."

She couldn't hear what was said on the other end, but she could imagine. Blah blah blah best wishes on your upcoming nuptials...

"Listen, I will see you tomorrow, right? Yeah, the rehearsal dinner." He glanced at his watch. "I'm supposed to be meeting Van for dinner tonight—some French place an hour from here—and I don't want to be late, so..."

Something Uncle Jerry said got a laugh out of Ned. Rosebud rolled her eyes. Something amusing about the joys of coping with Vanessa, no doubt.

But Ned looked distracted as he spun back around, still holding the receiver. He peered at the bed, where the shirt he'd been wearing, the one that had landed on Rosebud, now lay flat. His expression grew even more perplexed. "Uncle Jerry, did you say there were stories about this place being..." He paused. "Haunted?"

Rosebud tried not to giggle. It was just the look on his face, as if someone were poking him with sticks and forcing him to ask that question. So Neddy boy was embarrassed to ask about things that went bump in the night. It was kind of sweet. Of course, she hadn't believed in ghosts, either. Until she became one.

"No, honestly, I'm a total skeptic," Ned said quickly into the phone. "I was starting to think there was something weird going on around here, but... Can't be. That would just be stupid."

He forced another laugh. "Aw, I'm sure you're right. Just stress from the wedding. You and Aunt Win always have known me better than anyone else."

Aw, how sweet. When she was young and desperate for guidance, it would've been nice to have a kindly aunt or uncle to turn to.

"Your support has meant everything to me, I want you to know that," Ned continued. "I know I've been strange lately. I never thought I was the marrying kind to start out with, so this is all..."

Ned paused, suddenly looking so gloomy it sent a little arrow right into Rosebud's heart. She should've been happy to hear he wasn't thrilled with the prospect of getting married, given how she felt about his bride and the fact that she was already hatching plans to ruin their nuptials. But his features were so woebegone she felt sorry for him.

"It's all new," he said finally. "Unexpected. Whatever. No, I'm great. Vanessa is great. The wedding will be great. Everything will be..."

She could finish that halfhearted sentiment for him. *Great.* Except it seemed they both knew that was a lie.

Ned said goodbye to his uncle and hung up the

phone, crossing quickly to the closet. It was obvious he was in a hurry to get dressed and get out of there.

"Wouldn't want to be late to meet the odious Vanessa," Rosebud murmured, watching as he pulled a shirt off a hanger. Now that was a shame, covering up all that male beauty. And she'd hardly seen anything yet.

He hustled into his clothes, put on a different belt, picked up his keys, ran a comb through his hair, and made tracks.

As soon as he was gone, Rosebud slipped down from the armoire, feeling oddly dejected. If she were being a dutiful honeymoon helper, she would've followed him, but she didn't see the point. After all, he'd told his uncle that he and Vanessa were going off the premises for dinner, and as Rosebud well knew, the good-time ghosts who haunted Miss Arlotta's establishment were not allowed to pass outside its doors. She had to stay here alone while Ned went off with his bride-to-be.

"And I didn't even get to see him naked below the waist," she said cynically. "Darn that Uncle Jerry, anyway."

There was nothing to be done about it. But as long as she was there, she might as well do a little snooping.

Hmm... He'd left his wallet on the dresser. It contained a license which permitted him to drive motor vehicles, and that gave her the interesting information that he was born in 1974. "I was born in 1874," she said happily. "Something else we have in common."

The wallet also held plenty of cash and several plastic rectangles with his name printed on them. She didn't quite have a grasp on those yet, but she knew they could substitute for money in today's world. She'd seen commercials on television. Still... It seemed odd he didn't take his money with him.

Ooh, goodie. He'd also left behind one of those small computer items which she liked so much. MBA? No, that wasn't it. The twenty-first century was chock full of acronyms, and she could never keep them straight.

"Personal something-or-other. Begins with P. PTA, maybe." Before she had a chance to get at it, a knock on the door interrupted her.

"Room service," someone called out. "Mr. Mulgrew? Are you in?"

Quickly she shoved the wallet and the PDA—oh, yes, PDA, that was it—into the top drawer and then flew back to her safe spot on the armoire. After another knock, the young man from room service let himself in, whistling some nondescript tune as he brought in a silver ice bucket and a bottle of wine. He set them up on the dresser, along with a small, square white envelope with Ned's name neatly written on the outside. And then he came back in with a bouquet of flowers arranged in a crystal vase. Red roses. Nice.

As soon as the boy was gone, Rosebud was at the dresser, pulling open the envelope and shamelessly examining the card. *"You've always been like a son to us, and we're here for you whenever you need us. Have a great stay at the Inn! Can't wait for the wedding. Love from Uncle Jerry and Aunt Win,"* she read. "Can't wait for the wedding? You may have to, Uncle Jerry and Aunt Win, if I have anything to say about it."

Rosebud quickly retrieved Ned's PDA and pushed

enough buttons to get it turned on. She found names and addresses, appointments, bank balance—a very healthy one—and important dates not to forget, including what he had sent in the way of gifts to whom for birthdays and anniversaries. Jerry and Edwina Foster, who must be the aunt and uncle, were in there, as were Mom, Dad, Vanessa and a pair of extra Westicotts who must be her parents.

It seemed Ned was organized as well as thoughtful. Very lawyerly in approach to names and dates, anyway. Vanessa's birthday was included, but their upcoming wedding date was not.

"Maybe that's something he wants to forget," Rosebud said hopefully.

As she hovered there in front of the mirror, she decided it looked strange for the PDA to be floating in the air all by itself. She really shouldn't. She wasn't supposed to. But...

The fact was, she was very good at materializing. She practiced all the time by herself in her nook in the attic, and nobody was the wiser. And here she had a mirror, where she could judge her handiwork. Who would ever know if she went 3-D in Ned's room while he was away?

As quickly as that, Rosebud flashed into place. Not in pieces, not from the bottom up or the top down, but boom, all at once, with the PDA balanced on her hand instead of floating.

"Not bad, Rose," she whispered, squinting through her wire-rimmed spectacles at her reflection. "Not bad at all."

After setting down the computer, she did a little turn

in front of Ned's dresser, taking a survey. The same long, dark ringlets she remembered, the same small, heart-shaped face, a paler shade than was currently fashionable, the same wide green eyes and the same slender body, looking very fetching, if she did say so herself, in the thin rosebud-embroidered chemise, corset and lacy knickers in which she'd passed over into the immortal world.

She removed her glasses and polished them, backing away from the mirror for a more complete look. Except for a few wavy lines down around her left ankle, she was totally three-dimensional.

"You are really getting good at this," she congratulated herself, concentrating and bringing her blurry ankle into sharper focus. Perfect.

It felt different being in Ned's room as a fully fleshed-out person, and she danced around a little, testing the hardwood and soft Oriental rug against her bare feet, enjoying the heady idea of being a real-live girl. She smelled Ned's soap, she took a few licks through her hair with his brush, and she couldn't resist picking up the knit shirt he'd left on the bed.

Draping it around her shoulders, Rosebud closed her eyes and inhaled Eau de Real Man, wrapping one sleeve tightly around her, pretending for just a moment that it was Ned's arm. Mmm... Ned's arm, holding her close. It was wonderful.

But then she heard the distinct sound of a key grinding in the lock and the door creaking open. Startled out of her fantasy, Rosebud whirled, her heart pounding.

"Who are you?" Ned demanded. He lounged there in the doorway, big as life and twice as scary. "What are you doing in my room?"

3

NED NARROWED HIS GAZE. She certainly didn't look like a burglar. What kind of burglar broke into a hotel room barefoot, wearing exotic, old-fashioned underwear, just to paw a shirt?

She was pretty enough, he'd give her that, with the long dark ringlets and the filmy, sexy little outfit. He'd never been into costumes or props when it came to sex, but he had to admit, the vintage virgin thing was definitely working for her. She was small and slender, but the tight corset cinched in her waist and thrust the pale, creamy mounds of her breasts up over the lacy edge of her top. All that clingy, gauzy white fabric, with the lines of her hips and her thighs visible through those crazy bloomers... It was a killer.

As he studied her, her lips parted slightly and she seemed to have difficulty finding enough air. She breathed unevenly, pitching her breasts that much farther over the edge, up and down, rubbing against the lace, making the picture even better. Or worse.

Okay, this was wrong. So wrong. On so many levels.

Ned rubbed a thumb against his forehead. He was getting married in a few days. To Vanessa. Now was not the time to be leering at strange women. Especially as strange as this one. He clenched his jaw, forcing himself to pull his gaze away from her delicious curves, focusing on her face.

Pretty eyes. Dangerous eyes. Wide and green, they sparkled with mystery and mischief, as if she were too smart, too innocent, and too *alive* to be ignored. It was an unusual mix. And why was she staring at him like that, her head tipped to one side, like he was an ice cream cone she was dying to lick? He couldn't recall ever being devoured by a woman's eyes like that. At least not in a good way. And this was very good.

Ned was, suddenly, totally turned on. As her hungry gaze flicked over him, he could feel his body harden in response.

No. He couldn't do this. *Find out who she is and get rid of her. Now. Before this gets any worse.*

"Did Chris send you?" he asked impatiently.

"Excuse me?" Her voice sounded husky and a little rusty, as if she hadn't used it in a while. She cleared her throat as she idled there, sort of twitching under his scrutiny. Yeah, well, he was feeling a little twitchy himself.

"My best man. Because if he sent you as a pre-bachelor party stripper or something, I'm sorry, but I'm not interested."

"Stripper?" It seemed to take her a second to comprehend the word or the concept. Then her eyes widened behind her wire-rimmed glasses. "You mean someone who takes her clothes off for money? Dancing around with no clothes? Heavens, no. *No.* Nothing like that."

Yeah, he didn't think so. Whatever she was, she

didn't look like a stripper. Not with glasses. "Okay, I give. Who are you?"

"Well, I'm the, uh, chambermaid," she said hastily.

"The chambermaid. So what are you doing with my shirt?"

"Oh." Blinking, she glanced at the garment draped over her arm and then back at him. "I was sent to fetch your cleaning, sir. Since this garment had been tossed willy-nilly on the bed, I assumed it was the article in question." She extended it toward him, holding it delicately by two fingers. "I did knock. But there was no answer. I reckoned you had gone out and I would just pop in and pick up the, er, item."

"I wanted my tuxedo cleaned," he said warily, advancing on her, still trying to figure her out. He jammed his hands in his pockets. Was it him, or was her vocabulary a little odd? *Fetch? Willy-nilly?* And *reckoned?* "I'm getting married on Friday. In it. So it needs to be cleaned."

"Of course." Awkwardly she scooted backward toward the bed and dropped his shirt there. Leaving a wide space between them, she made a move toward the closet, offering, "I'll just get your tuxedo, then."

Ned shook his head. He still wasn't buying this. "Why are you dressed like that? I mean, if you're the maid, why not a uniform instead of—" How was he going to describe what she was wearing? He didn't even try, just broke off and let his sentence hang there, unfinished.

"This is my uniform," she answered quickly. "We all dress like this."

"All the maids?" he asked, raising an eyebrow at

that one. How did any new groom stay faithful for more than five minutes if the maid romping around his room looked like this? More to the point, why would any bride choose the Inn if it had that kind of competition?

"They want us to resemble the ladies who worked here back in the old days." She busied herself trying to ease his tuxedo out of the closet. With the jacket in one hand and the pants in the other, she added, "You know, the soiled doves."

"The what?"

"Soiled doves? Ladies of ill repute?"

Ned could only shake his head.

"Hookers," she said flatly. She blushed a becoming shade of pink. "The Inn was a bordello back in 1895, chock full of hookers. So I am wearing a historical costume like what they wore then. You know, for atmosphere. And, um, verisimilitude."

Now he was sure she was no stripper. Verisimilitude? Besides, it made her blush to say *hooker*. "What's your name?" he asked, intrigued. He told himself he'd only asked in case he needed to check her out with housekeeping or report this crazy incident later.

She hesitated. After a moment, she said simply, "Rose." She smiled, as if she were waiting for a reaction.

He found himself grinning back at her, although he had no idea why. It was just that her smile was infectious and saucy, and it was impossible not to return it. Even if she was nuttier than a fruitcake.

As she turned back to the tux, Ned ran a hand through his hair. None of this made sense. Least of all the fact that it felt like a gift when all she did was tell him her name or offer a smile.

Trying to shake it off, he went the opposite direction, to the dresser, to take a look at the flowers and wine that had shown up while he was out. The card said they were from his aunt and uncle, who said they couldn't wait for the wedding. *His* wedding. *Oh, man. What a mess.* But he had other things to think about right now. Like the living, breathing woman in his room who happened to be dressed as if she were a model for Victoria's Secret. *Queen* Victoria's Secret.

"Rose, did you drop these off?" he asked, holding up the card from the flowers. At least that would account for her being there.

"Oh, *those.* Why, yes. Yes, I did." Her eyes were wide and innocent as she continued. "I delivered the roses and the wine, set them up right there, pretty as you please, and then I set out to collect the cleaning, when, of course, I had a slight mishap. By taking the, uh, shirt instead of the tuxedo. But I shall endeavor to do better in future."

"You shall?" he asked, wondering what planet he'd landed on.

"As your chambermaid, I mean." She sent him a determined smile and adopted a singsong, cheery tone. "I shall perform the usual chambermaid duties of cleaning the room and plumping your pillows and bringing extra towels and making sure you have enough of the tiny soaps and shampoo bottles which we offer here at the Inn. I can also procure a toothbrush or razor if you need one. We believe in personal service here at the Inn. As your chambermaid, you may think of me as Johnny-on-the-Spot."

Johnny-on-the-Spot, huh? He had to admit, she did hit the spot. In a way that made him very uneasy.

Ned wondered suddenly whether it was his attraction to her that had made him suspicious right from the beginning. If you took a groom with cold feet and then threw a sexy, tempting (and slightly odd) woman at him, it would be natural for him to fixate on her rather than looking at what was really going on with himself. So maybe he'd created a mystery where there was none, as a distraction.

Because wasn't the easiest explanation that she really *was* the maid?

"Thank you, Rose," Ned offered, feeling a little ashamed of himself. "I appreciate the service."

He should probably tip her. He wondered what he had in the way of bills and how much he should tip, especially after he'd insulted her by asking if she was a stripper.

It occurred to him that the maids here probably got very good tips with those outfits. He patted his pockets. Oh, his wallet. That was why he'd come back to his room, after all, because he'd forgotten his wallet.

"That's weird," he said absently. His wallet wasn't on the dresser with the coins and keys where he'd left it. His Blackberry was there, but it was switched on. He didn't remember using it. And where was his wallet?

He glanced at Rose, who was studiously draping his tux across her outstretched arms. Maybe his missing wallet explained Rose's presence after all. Maybe she was a petty thief who'd taken his wallet and played with his Blackberry. Maybe he'd interrupted her before she could steal it, too, and she'd had no choice but to stick it back on the dresser. Not much place to hide it considering what she was wearing.

"Rose, while you've been here, did you see a wallet?" he asked quietly, keeping his gaze fixed on her.

"I'm afraid not." Her expression was serene and unconcerned, without a hint of guilt. "I know when I can't find something, I usually discover I left it in a pocket or a drawer. Did you check your trousers? Your jacket? The drawers?"

"No, I didn't, but..." He was wearing the same pants and he hadn't had on a jacket, so that wasn't it. To look like a good sport, he wrenched open the top dresser drawer, positive the wallet wouldn't be there. But it was. Huh? Hastily he checked it. As far as he could tell, all his cash and credit cards were where they should be.

"Oh, did you find it? I'm glad I suggested that," she put in brightly.

Once again, he was baffled and bewildered. He pulled out a twenty to offer as a tip. But then he stopped.

He couldn't ever remembering leaving his wallet in a drawer. He always left his keys, his change and his wallet on his dresser at home, or on top of the dresser or the desk if he was traveling. And he was practically positive he hadn't used the PDA. Touches from invisible hands on the stairs, his clothes flapping around of their own accord, his wallet moved, his Blackberry turned on... What in the world was going on around here?

With his tux clutched close, Rose marched toward the door. But Ned stepped into her path.

"Rose," he said firmly, "you need to tell me what this is all about." He took her by the shoulders, feeling almost a shock of recognition and electricity as his fingers met her skin. *Whoa.*

That was a lot from a simple touch, especially since he hadn't been trying to create sparks, just block her exit. Unable to pull back, he rubbed his thumb around the curve of her shoulder, tracing the ruffled strap of her camisole, easing it down, leaving her whole shoulder bare. *Whoa.*

Rose stood very still, not moving closer but not moving away, either. "I—I don't know what you mean," she managed, in a sexy, husky whisper.

He was standing so close he could see right down the front of her shirt. Bad move. With one strap down, there was way too much skin in full view, her breasts curving sweetly against the tiny rosebuds embroidered around the lacy edge, threatening to tumble out completely. His fingers itched to make good on the threat.

Determined not to give in, he focused on her eyes and pushed on with what he wanted to say, getting more frustrated by the second. "You can't be the maid," he argued. "You're barefoot. You're almost naked. I'm not stupid, Rose. You *can't* be the maid."

She chewed on her lip, and he could see she was trying to decide what to say. Or maybe what lie to come up with next. But she smelled faintly of roses, her skin felt like heaven in his hands, and Ned knew he didn't care if she never told him the truth.

Oh, Lord. That was all he needed, a ridiculous attraction to a woman he knew nothing about. But every time his conscious mind told him to stop acting like a lunatic, something else pushed him back under her spell.

Right now, he knew she was soft and warm under his hands, that her smiles made him feel alive, that his touch made her tremble. Whoever she was, whatever she was doing here, there was some bizarre, cosmic connection between the two of them. Like they were lashed together with a bolt of lightning.

Bolt of lightning? What was wrong with him? He wasn't the kind of guy who thought about things like that. Ever.

This was freaky. Ned Mulgrew was a practical, no-nonsense lawyer. He believed in logic and reason, not kismet. His life and his career were planned out, down to the last detail. He was not the kind of person who ever went near bolts of lightning.

"I'm sorry," she murmured. She gazed up at him through dark, thick lashes. Her green eyes were filled with guilt and longing. "I know I shouldn't. I am going to be in so much trouble. But I can't help it."

"Help what?"

He barely got the words out before she stretched up on her tiptoes, tangled her arms around the back of his neck, let his tuxedo fall to the floor like so much unwanted baggage, and pressed her hot, moist, open mouth into his.

Ned had kissed a lot of women in his time, but nothing like this. It was like jumping into the deep, dark end of the pool. Like everything he'd ever wanted, right there where he could taste it.

He pulled her hard into his embrace, slanting his mouth over hers, plunging deeper. Lifting her completely off the ground, he fitted her body to his. He couldn't get close enough. A tiny moan of pleasure escaped her lips, and that only made it worse somehow.

This had to be the biggest mistake he'd ever made in his life. And he didn't care.

Collision course with...something. He just didn't know what. But if he didn't have her in the next five minutes, he thought he might die.

Boom, boom, boom.

Confused, Ned stumbled backward, almost dropping her. Was that his heart? No, it was the door. Someone was pounding on the door to his room.

"Ned? Are you in there? What's taking so long?"

Oh, God. Vanessa.

Ned swore under his breath, but Rose was already disconnecting herself and edging away from him.

"Rose, I—"

"It's okay," she interrupted. She smiled again, patting him on the cheek and gently pushing him toward the door. "Thank you for the kiss, Ned. Thank you so much. Now go ahead and answer."

How could she be so calm? His mind was still reeling with the implications of what had just happened, while his body lagged behind in hot-to-trot mode. He was a sane, rational man, and this stuff...was neither.

Making out with the chambermaid while his fiancée pounded on the door? It was like a cheap sex farce and not at all like his well-ordered life.

Boom. Boom. Boom.

"Open this door, Ned!"

"How am I going to explain this to Vanessa? How am I going to explain this to myself?" he muttered, as he swung open the door.

At least the sight of her furious face cooled his ardor. Quickly.

"What's going on?" Vanessa demanded. "You got the wallet, right?"

"It's on the dresser. It just took a while to find it." He shook his head and braced himself in the doorframe, hopefully blocking her view. "I can't figure it out. I left it in the drawer, and I never do that."

"Okay, well, let's get it and go." She frowned, ducking under his arm and storming full speed ahead into his room.

"Van, don't—" But it was too late. She was in.

Defeated, Ned sagged against the wall, waiting for the explosion that was going to happen as soon as Vanessa caught a glimpse of Rose and her skimpy lingerie.

Except there was no explosion.

He turned. Vanessa picked his wallet up off the vanity and tossed it in his direction. "Catch." He caught it. "What's wrong?" she asked as she sauntered back around him, leading the way into the hall. "You look like you've seen a ghost."

Actually, it was the opposite. He didn't see anything. Or anyone. So where the hell had Rose disappeared to?

"YOU *KISSED* HIM?" Miss Arlotta thundered. "What in tarnation were you thinking, Rosebud?"

"I hadn't kissed a man in 109 years!" she protested, still not appreciating being yanked up to the attic like a rag doll. She had been leaving his room, anyway. There was no need for all the drama. And how did Miss A do that, anyway? Rosebud wished she knew that trick. "When you're starving for 109 years and someone dangles a piece of fried chicken in front of you, you just grab it. Don't you?"

The boss's face said it all. Disgust.

Rosebud added darkly, "I couldn't help it."

"You better help it, missy. You know the rules."

"Yes, but..." But what? But nothing. She did know the rules. She had no excuse, no defense. And if she didn't come up with something quickly, her boss would take Ned away and banish her to the wine cellar or something. She couldn't let that happen. Improvising, she said, "It was part of my plan, to get him stirred up and, and, well, *eager* for his bride."

Miss Arlotta raised one thin platinum eyebrow, indicating she was not fooled by that ploy.

"They're in separate rooms," Rosebud went on. "I'm working at a serious disadvantage. I thought..." She paused. "I thought maybe if I got him a little heated up and then disappeared he would turn to his fiancée."

Still nothing but disapproval and disbelief radiated from the boss.

Rosebud snapped, "You know yourself that every other woman here has kissed at least one groom!"

"Yeah, well, maybe," the madam said slowly. She shook her tightly coiffed head. "But one more transgression like that, and you will be yanked off this case so fast it will make your spectacles spin to the back of your head."

Looking all smug and superior, the Countess sidled closer. She crossed her arms over her scarlet silk robe. "I vould be heppy to tek dis couple," she announced. She was really laying the accent on thick tonight. It reminded Rosebud of a cartoon she'd seen, something with a moose and a squirrel. The villainess in it had sounded just like the Countess. "Before two minutes passes, dey vill be zo hot, one for de ozer, steam vill rise from de bed."

That woman was as phony as a three-dollar bill. There was no way Rosebud was going to stand by and let the Countess get her greedy paws on sweet Ned. "That won't be necessary, Countess. No more kisses for me. Not even one."

"Are you zzzure, Leetle Rosebud?"

"Yes," Rosebud snapped. She hated being called "Little Rosebud." "I'm positive."

"All right, all right, enough," Miss A declared. "This is still Rosebud's assignment. For now." In a sharper tone, she added, "But you'd better shape up. Remember, your bride and groom love each other. They are affianced and headed for holy matrimony! Don't be messin' with that!"

"I won't. I'll be good. I'll be perfect."

"Stay away from him," Miss A ordered. "In the morning, you better be doggin' that bride's every step. Your job is to put some giddy-up in her gallop, remember? Don't let me down, Rosebud."

"Right." She pressed her lips together, trying to forget what it had felt like when she kissed Ned. So swoony. So yummy. So devastatingly right. If only she could try it again, only longer this time.

Uh-oh. She was in so much trouble. And she just couldn't seem to help herself.

Wednesday morning

NED WAS DREAMING about a mysterious woman in white. She had dark hair, but she wasn't Vanessa. This one was softer, her hair loose and long, and she was barefoot. She was wearing the most tantalizing outfit, revealing more than it hid, and yet he couldn't quite see her, couldn't quite make out where the cool, transparent fabric ended and her warm flesh began.

She smiled and laughed, beckoning to him, dancing a step farther away. He wanted her so badly his whole body ached, but every time he reached for her, she eluded him. Giggling, teasing, darting just out of range...

She slipped past him, but he caught one flimsy, lacy panel of her dress, and this time he held on tight. Triumphant, he wrapped the clingy fabric around his fist, hauling her closer, baring her leg and thigh up to the waist, forcing her flush up against him. He could see the anticipation in her sparkling emerald eyes, hear the shaky rasp of her breath, feel how she quivered with excitement.

He smiled. He'd caught her now, and she was all his....

The phone rang insistently across the room, jolting him out of his dream. Damn it. Ned sat up, frustrated and alone, with a fistful of bedsheet. White, lace-edged sheet. So much for catching the woman in white.

He shook his head. How much was a dream and how much was reality? Had there ever been a woman in his room last night? Had she really kissed him? Or was he losing his mind?

And the phone just kept ringing. "Yeah, yeah, I'm coming." Dragging the sheet with him, Ned padded over to the dresser and picked up the phone. "Hello," he mumbled.

"Hey, kid, it's Dad," he heard in his ear. "You sound like you just woke up. Kind of late, isn't it?"

"What time is it?"

"Ten."

"Ten o'clock?" He shook his head hard to clear away the cobwebs. He was used to being up by six o'clock every morning to give him time in the gym before he had to be at the law firm.

"Must've been a late night," his father said with a knowing chuckle.

Yeah, he wished. Instead of doing anything exciting, he'd languished over a dull dinner with Vanessa, saying "uh-huh" whenever there was a pause during her list of all the things that still needed to be done before the wedding. He'd pretended to listen, but he couldn't keep his mind off the mysterious maid and that mind-blowing kiss. Vanessa hadn't seemed to notice he wasn't paying attention, so he supposed it was a case of no harm, no foul. Even though he still felt guilty.

The guilt probably explained the dream. Except that hadn't felt like guilt. It was way too good for that.

"Must be the mountain air," he joked. "Or the altitude. Clogging my brain."

"Listen, Ned, I'm downstairs in the lobby. I can't check in yet. Want to meet me for a cup of coffee, breakfast, whatever, down in the hotel restaurant? Vanessa can come, too, if she's free."

"Nah, she's tied up all day checking out the flowers and the menu for the rehearsal dinner." Vanessa was not going to allow any detail to go unchecked. Not to mention double- and triple-checked. The rehearsal dinner wasn't even her responsibility, but she didn't care. She was on top of it and she was going to stomp it into submission. "Where's Mom?"

"She'll be up later today. I thought I'd come on ahead and see if you needed anything." His dad finished up with a hearty, "Wouldn't want there to be any surprises on your big day."

"Yeah, wouldn't want that." Vanessa and his father were clearly on the same page. For that matter, everybody seemed a lot more anxious for this wedding than he was. Well, except his mother. She wasn't crazy about Vanessa. She kept her mouth shut, deferring to his father as usual, but he could tell. He shook his head. He'd never anticipated he would be following his parents' path, with a marriage that was more like a business arrangement, and yet here he was. He mumbled, "Give me time to jump in the shower and I'll be right down."

Ned made his shower extra-cold, but it didn't seem to help. All he could think about was that dream and the sexy little chambermaid in it. Was she a convenient excuse *not* to think about his wedding? A last-gasp sexual fantasy stemming from a fear of committing himself to marriage?

It had been a long time since he took that Law and Psychiatry class. About all he knew at the moment was that he probably wasn't crazy enough to be committed. Yet. He felt sure his aunt, well-known psychologist Edwina Mulgrew Foster, could come up with plenty of diagnoses for his current problem. Not that he was going to ask her.

"You know, the most logical explanation is that Rose was just somebody in the wrong place at the wrong time. She was probably not a complete figment of your imagination. It was late and you were tired, and you imagined that she and her outfit were a lot more..." He searched for the right word. When it came to Rose and the impact of what she was wearing, *a lot more* pretty much summed it up. "So your mind made her out to be something amazing, when in the clear light of day, you would've known she was pretty much like any other girl."

Yeah, that sounded about right, he decided as he jogged down the main staircase to the restaurant. Pretty much like any other girl.

He hadn't been in the restaurant before, but it was posh and comfortable. It was also fairly empty at the moment. He was late for breakfast but early for lunch, apparently. As Ned ambled in the doorway, he didn't see his father, but he did see a large open menu on a stand, letting him know that the restaurant was called The Golden Rule. Odd name for a restaurant. It was also not a reminder he needed at the moment.

After all, the Golden Rule was all about "Do unto

others," when just last night he had been on the verge
of doing something very ugly unto his fiancée. Like
cheating, for example.

"It was one kiss. That doesn't make me a cheater,"
he told himself as he spotted his dad sitting at a table
over by the window.

It was oddly comforting to see a familiar face. He
and his father weren't exactly close—he'd always gravitated toward Aunt Win, his father's sister, and her
husband Jerry, when he craved the warmth of a
home—but in the midst of insanity, tall, broad-
shouldered Edmund John Mulgrew III, nicknamed
Jack to distinguish him from the others, was a safe, reliable lifeboat.

The senior Mulgrew rose and shook Ned's hand,
slapping him fondly on the shoulder. "You look good,
kid. Everything going okay so far?"

"Yeah, sure. You know Vanessa." He tried to smile.
"Everything works like a well-oiled machine. She
won't allow anything else."

"Exactly. That's why she's perfect for you, Ned.
You're the same way."

"At least I used to be," he said under his breath.

As he sat down, a waitress arrived to pour him a cup
of coffee and hand him a menu. She was wearing a
long black skirt and a white blouse with the biggest,
puffiest sleeves he'd ever seen. Her hair was pulled
back into a loose bun, and she had a cameo pinned at
her throat. He wasn't much for women's clothes, but
even he could tell she was supposed to look like she'd
just walked out of another century.

So maybe the employees here really did dress in historical costumes. Hers wasn't nearly as revealing as the chambermaid's, however. Maybe they waited till after dark to spring the risqué stuff.

"So," his father said briskly, "everything on track for the merger?"

Ned's response was automatic. "The board meeting is scheduled for the first of the month. Tom Westicott will recommend that his directors accept your terms, and the merger should go off without a hitch." He winced as he took a healthy gulp of coffee. Hot. Very hot.

"All the t's crossed and the i's dotted?" Jack Mulgrew tapped his spoon nervously against his saucer. "We need this merger, Ned."

"Yes, Dad, I'm well aware of that. And, yes, everything is set. That is my area of expertise, you know." He'd been doing mergers and acquisitions at the law firm for a few years now. Not only was he good at it, but he was actually considered a "rainmaker," someone who brought in valuable business.

So it was normal for him to work on this Mulgrew-Westicott merger. But how his wedding and the two companies merging had wound up tied together he still didn't know. Somehow his marriage proposal had ended up part of the same Fourth of July party where the two fathers hashed out the idea of merging Mulgrew Media and Westicott Cable Systems. Growing up, moving on, companies merging, families combining... Why not?

"Come on, Ned. It makes perfect sense and you know it," his dad argued. "It's not like somebody has to twist your arm. Vanessa is beautiful and classy.

She's exactly what you need in a wife. You've been dating for two years. It's past time for you to get married and start a family."

"Wouldn't want to keep Edmund John Mulgrew V waiting."

"Ned," his father began in an ominous tone, but the waitress returned to see if anyone wanted to order anything, and he broke off.

Ned welcomed the opportunity to steer the conversation away from future generations of Mulgrews, so he smiled up at the waitress. "I couldn't help but notice your outfit. Do all of the hotel employees wear historical costumes?"

"That depends on what you mean by costumes," she said as she topped off his coffee. "Most of us do wear uniforms that reflect the 1890s. The appeal of the Inn is its unique history, after all."

"It's a fascinating place," he noted, as his father looked on, utterly mystified.

"Well, if you want to know more about the history, you'll need to drop by the small parlor, off the main lobby," she told him with enthusiasm. "Back in 1895, it was a small, private parlor for high rollers who came to visit the bordello. Now it's been restored as nearly as we can get it to its original condition. There are even photos there of the madam and her girls."

"Her girls?" Ned teased. "You mean the soiled doves?"

She laughed. "Sounds like you already know the history."

"But what about ghosts?" he asked. "I hear the Inn is haunted."

The waitress dipped closer to the table. In a confidential tone, she whispered, "I've never seen or heard anything weird myself. But a lot of people have claimed to hear the piano playing all by itself in the historical parlor or curtains waving for no reason. And they also say sometimes you can see the ladies wearing hardly anything hanging over the balcony on the roof."

"Ned?" Jack Mulgrew interrupted impatiently. "Is there a reason for all this chitchat?"

"I find it interesting."

"What we were discussing before was *important.*" He shook his head darkly, and the waitress took that as her cue to scoot away. "You are on the brink of the rest of your life, Ned. You need to focus on Vanessa and the merger. You stand to make a few million yourself, just for your shares in M2. That's a nice reason to get married all by itself."

"I know, Dad, but..." But the truth was, he couldn't stop thinking about one sultry little chambermaid and her vintage lingerie.

"I don't know what's gotten into you," his dad continued, sounding even more unhappy. "You're not acting like yourself at all. You wanted this wedding. What's changed?"

"Nothing has changed," he said wearily. He met his father's gaze. "I guess I'm just wondering if there shouldn't be more than this when you marry someone."

"More than what? Vanessa will be a major asset to you and to this family." The elder Mulgrew sighed, adopting a more kindly expression. "Every man gets a little nervous before he says 'I Do.' Ball and chain and all that. It's normal."

"I'm sure you're right."

"Keep focused, okay?" His dad reached across to knock him on the arm. "Vanessa is a smart cookie, and she'll know if something's wrong. You've got the rehearsal dinner tonight and the bachelor party tomorrow, right? Just keep putting one foot in front of the other and you'll be married before you know it."

"That's what I'm afraid of."

ROSEBUD HOVERED behind a potted palm, shamelessly eavesdropping. "I don't think I like Dear Old Dad," she decided, keeping her words inaudible. "He reminds me of Edmund."

What was it he'd said? Rehearsal dinner tonight and bachelor party tomorrow.

"Plenty of opportunities for me to prove to Ned that Vanessa is not the right woman for him." Rosebud smiled as she floated up through the ceiling of The Golden Rule. "Plenty of opportunities."

4

Wednesday evening

THE ASSEMBLED GUESTS were already on their salads by the time Rosebud showed up at the rehearsal dinner. Well, everyone except Vanessa. Rosebud ran into her first, where she stood over by the door, loudly chattering on her cell phone, completely ignoring her guests.

Rosebud shook her head. That Vanessa. Could she be any more annoying?

As Rosebud swooped past Vanessa and scoped out the long tables in the private dining room, she quickly spied Ned. *Oh, dear.* She was all aflutter. Her pulse raced, her breath got shaky, and she felt flushed and hot. Or maybe she was just hovering too close to all the candles.

Fanning herself, she backed away from the candelabras, taking refuge behind Ned's chair. Nope, not the candles. The heat she felt was radiating from Ned. He looked luscious in that suit and tie. So luscious she was dying to peel him out of it.

"I shouldn't have kissed him," she realized woefully. "Now I have a hankering to kiss him again. And again. Maybe a few hundred times."

It wasn't her fault that the blue of his dress shirt brought out the blue in his eyes, or that he wore his clothes with such easy grace. It wasn't her fault he was so dashing and adorable.

Too bad she'd promised not to kiss him again. But now that she thought about it, she hadn't actually promised not to *touch* him again. Touching was perfectly acceptable, wasn't it? She inched a little closer.

A mature brunette who must be Vanessa's mother sat on his right, and Rosebud eased herself on that side of him, watching, not making physical contact, just breathing him in for a second or two. But she couldn't help taking it further.

With one hand ever-so-lightly balanced on his shoulder, Rosebud bent in near enough to breathe on him, to trace a finger along the neckline of his shirt, then up and around the curve of his ear. Poor baby. Hot color began to creep up from his collar, giving him the most attractive pinkish hue, and a small tic appeared in his hard-clenched jaw.

With her head tipped next to his, Rosebud let a long tendril of her dark hair sweep over the front of him, tickling his shirt, pooling in his lap. The tic got worse.

She smiled. It was such fun to mess with Ned. As long as he was handy, why not?

Still, since he would only be at the hotel for a few days, she was a bit peeved she'd had to waste most of her time without even seeing him. It was downright maddening. After all, she could've spent today lounging around his room, watching him dress and undress some more. Maybe even supervised his bath.

Rosebud had to clamp down hard not to make a little *ooh* sound just thinking of Ned naked in a bathtub. Now that would've been worth the price of admission.

But she hadn't had a choice. She'd had to stay away. Miss Arlotta wanted to see concrete evidence—plans, schedules, charts—of what she intended to do to Vanessa. Or, rather, *for* Vanessa. Since what she had up her sleeve wasn't exactly legit, she had no intention of sharing it with Miss A.

Her ideas didn't amount to much, anyway. Not one of her more inspired efforts, the plan so far included a series of little tricks, the usual assortment of appearing, disappearing and misplaced items, maybe a trip or a pratfall or a "Boo!" or two, designed to surprise and annoy Vanessa and provoke her into showing her true colors as an ill-tempered, self-absorbed twit.

But it wouldn't do to let Miss Arlotta know any of that. So all day Rosebud pretended she had other, more virtuous schemes afoot, dutifully following Vanessa around, taking notes, pretending to be hard at work, lying low till it was safe to come out and launch the real barrage of tricks. She'd even witnessed the alleged rehearsal, which consisted of Vanessa telling the few people who showed up that there wasn't going to be a rehearsal because "this isn't rocket science, people," that she had handouts for them which they should study before the ceremony.

As far as Rosebud was concerned, all it did was convince her even more that Vanessa was a pain in the derriere, and not nearly good enough for Ned.

"I'm saving Ned from a fate worse than death," Rosebud murmured, feeling self-righteous and secure in her mission. "I am *saving* him."

Now if only she could persuade Miss Arlotta of that. Sometimes the boss could be so single-minded. "Oh, well. Rules were made to be broken," she said under her breath. Not every bride and groom were destined to stay together if they weren't the right bride and groom. Or at least not the right *bride*. Surely Miss Arlotta would see that.

Luckily, Glory and Desdemoaner were providing a major distraction at this very moment. It seemed the "Wee Willie Winkie" groom did not enjoy hearing ghostly giggles while he tried to perform, and those two couldn't help but dissolve into howls every time he took off his pants. Glory and Des were in big trouble over that one. For Miss Arlotta, righting Wee Willie's honeymoon woes was more pressing at the moment than anything Rosebud was up to.

Thank goodness. Hmmm... Now that she thought about it, *goodness* and Ned did not seem to go together. When she looked at him, *badness* seemed like a much better choice.

Carelessly twisting herself around him, Rosebud hovered close enough to breathe a few hot puffs of air in his left ear. She whispered, "Goodness has nothing to do with it, does it, Ned?" Touching the tip of her tongue to his irresistible earlobe, she said huskily, "'Cause bad is lots more fun."

He jumped, his eyes wide, dropping his salad fork onto his plate with a clatter. "What?" he said out loud, turning to the woman on his left. "Mom? Did you just say something to me?"

"No." She looked worried. "Ned, are you all right?"

"Yes, fine. I just..." He shook his head. "I heard 'Goodness has nothing to do with it.' In my ear. It was so clear. Like earphones. And then..." He blushed again. "Never mind."

His mother leaned over and set her palm against his forehead. "You're a little hot. Are you running a fever, do you think?"

"I'm fine," he insisted.

"But you're hearing voices?" Mrs. Mulgrew spoke softly, but her alarm came through loud and clear. "Voices quoting lines from old movies?"

"Is it? From a movie? I don't know. I..." But he didn't finish that thought.

"Maybe you heard some kind of echo from Vanessa's cell phone," his mother suggested. "She's been on the phone forever."

"Right. Cell phone echo. I'm sure that's it."

But he looked rattled, and so did his mother. Rosebud retreated to the other side of the table, chewing on her thumbnail. Clearly she'd gone too far. She was supposed to be making Vanessa look bad, not Ned. Besides, she liked him. She liked him a lot. She didn't want him getting carted off to the loony bin.

So that thing about goodness was a line from a movie? Oh, wait. She remembered now. It *was* from a movie, something in black and white with that voluptuous lady who resembled Miss Arlotta. Mae West. Bad time, though, to remember Miss A, considering Rosebud was wafting around the dining room licking the groom and whispering incendiary phrases in his ear. If she got caught...

Licking and whispering didn't count as kissing, did they? Technically?

"All right, all right," she grumbled. "If I can't kiss

him, I suppose I shouldn't be licking him, either. More's the pity. But I reserve the right to engage in incendiary whispering."

Incendiary... Hmmm... It occurred to her that the omnipresent candelabras might be useful and might get her scheme back on track. Maybe she could pitch Vanessa into a candle and set her nasty little scarlet silk dress on fire. Then when the bride was shrieking and running for the exit, Rosebud could claim that she'd hatched it as a way to get Vanessa off the phone and for Ned to act like a hero when he saved his bride. If Vanessa went up in a ball of flame, Rosebud could just shrug and say, "Gee, what a shame! I had no idea that would happen."

But on the other hand... She was supposed to have learned in the past 109 years that her most impetuous ideas were usually her worst ones. As she thought about it, fire was awfully hard to control. Probably best to avoid flame-throwing at this juncture.

Hmmm... Rosebud circled the table, scrutinizing the guests. Even though she was champing at the bit to make mischief, she was still really curious about Ned's friends and relatives. She was getting a more complete picture of him as she figured out who was who.

She already knew his mother was the one sitting next to him, loyally patting his hand and telling him to relax, that everything would be fine. She seemed sweet. Rosebud tipped her head to the side, considering. Mrs. Mulgrew was well dressed, personable and she'd already sent a dubious glance or two Vanessa's way, when the bride-to-be had finally deigned to join them at the table after tucking her tiny cell phone back into her red leather purse. Yes, Rosebud definitely liked his mother.

His father... Not very much. He was seated next to his future daughter-in-law, and he was so attentive and charming. He kept complimenting the odious Vanessa on this and that—her manicure, her jewelry, the hideous dress—until it was apparent he was overdoing it.

"He is too much like Edmund," Rosebud decided. "Ned's like Edmund in all the good ways."

The guests at the second table included a less grumpy, slightly rounder version of Vanessa, who was identified as her younger sister and the matron of honor. The rest of that table consisted of the other members of the wedding party and their spouses. Two more bridesmaids, a best man who was rather attractive and a pair of handsome groomsmen rounded out the table. All married, all respectable. All dull.

As she eavesdropped, Rosebud caught snippets of conversation about 401k's and ERA's, athletic clubs, Atkins versus South Beach, whatever that meant, as well as chitchat about whose children attended the better nursery school.

Most of them looked as bored as she felt listening to them.

As for the older generation... There was an elderly woman who must be a Westicott grandparent, judging by the beady eyes and sharp, ferretlike features she shared with all the other Westicotts in attendance. Vanessa's mother was pretty and she was certainly dressed to the nines, but she hadn't said one word all evening, while Mr. Westicott kept yapping across the table at Ned about the proposed merger even though Ned was obviously tuning out.

Poor Ned. He murmured "Mmm-hmm" and sipped from his wineglass at appropriate intervals. But then his gaze seemed to sweep the room, a bit anxious, maybe expectant, as if he were waiting for something. Or perhaps someone.

"Maybe me?" Rosebud wondered. "Not now, Ned. Not here. But wait."

Besides Ned and his mother, the only people she liked at first sight were down at the end. They actually ate their food with gusto instead of picking at it, and they had a lively conversation going with Mrs. Mulgrew on the subject of movies and books. Rosebud gravitated to that direction.

"Jerry, you can't tell me your favorite movie is *The Matrix Reloaded*," Ned's mother said with a laugh. "I hated it. Absolutely hated it. What did you think, Win?"

Ah, so these two were Uncle Jerry and Aunt Edwina. Nice people. Yes, she liked them, she decided, making note of some of the movie titles they mentioned that sounded like they'd suit her taste. Once Ned left...

Ouch. Rosebud felt a strong, swift pang, realizing that very soon, whether she saved him from Vanessa or not, Ned would leave the Inn. Leave!

He would pack up his bags and vanish from her life forever. And she couldn't follow, couldn't possibly leave the Inn. It wasn't allowed. She would be left all alone with her DVDs and her battered books, the same as before. Once upon a time, *Lady Chatterley's Lover* and a Colin Firth movie had been enough to get her through the day. But now?

Now that she'd met Ned... Now that she'd kissed Ned... *Oh, heavens!* The body that hadn't been touched in 109 years suddenly pulsed with needs and desires.

Just that one kiss was better than the birthday when her father gave her a pony, better than her secret trysts with Edmund, better than spinning every newlywed in the Inn around in their beds.

Oh, dear. After this, after Ned left and took all the color and light, all the shivers and yearnings, with him, how could she ever go back to the way things had been? But what choice did she have? Seduce Ned now, tonight, so that she would at least have memories to keep her warm? Or stay away so that she wouldn't have memories haunting her?

Once Ned left, she'd have to find some way to return to being cantankerous, uncooperative Rosebud, the lonely ghost who tried her darnedest to stay away from other people's honeymoons. She was the one ghost in the place who had no interest in moving on to the Big Picnic in the Sky, and so she was stuck here with the status quo. Without Ned.

That thought was positively depressing.

Uh-oh. Ned was looking right at her. He didn't know she was there, of course, but he was gazing at the spot where she was standing, right between his aunt and uncle, and he had this intriguing half smile on his face. If she hadn't known better, she might've thought she was visible, that his eyes were meeting hers, that his smile was meant just for her. Rosebud felt her own lips curve into a smile, too. It was impossible to stay depressed when Ned was looking at her like that.

So what if he would only be here for a few days? She would savor every minute. They would still be—far and away—the best days she'd spent in the past 109 years.

"Sometimes you have to throw away the rules and grab for what you want," she said recklessly. "Can you hear me, Ned? Throw away the rules. Throw away your fiancée. Grab for me."

"Ned?" His mother nervously tapped him on the arm. She dropped her voice. "Ned, you're staring at an empty space. Not just staring, but smiling. You're starting to scare me. Are you okay?"

He pulled his gaze away from Rosebud. She could see him retreat, blink, come back to reality.

"Sure, I'm fine," he mumbled, staring down into his lap and studiously rearranging his napkin.

But Rosebud knew better. "There is a connection between us, Ned," she said softly. "You know I'm here. Whether you want to admit it or not."

But he didn't lift his head.

Her concentration was interrupted by the waiters bringing dessert trays. One of the waiters walked right through her invisible form, which rattled his tray and upset her equilibrium, but she tried to get past it.

Vanessa got first choice, but she waved away the whole tray, concentrating on her wine. For some reason, that really annoyed Rosebud. Vanessa had the opportunity to dip into chocolate mousse and carrot cake with cream cheese frosting, not to mention a lovely strawberry tart, and she preferred to suck down a plain white wine she herself had proclaimed mediocre.

Even more maddening, she had the chance to make mad, passionate love to Ned every night, and she chose to sleep in that beautiful suite alone.

Conversation dimmed around the table as the others focused on dessert, but then the best man, a good-looking guy named Chris, rose and announced that he thought they should try to liven up the proceedings. He had already proposed a toast or two, and he raised his glass again.

"To my friend Ned," he said with a grin. "I've known you forever, Ned. We made it through under-grad, we made it through law school, we made it through keggers and final exams and more girlfriends than either of us is ever going to admit."

Chris's wife poked him with her elbow, but he kept going. "So here's to Ned," he offered, "who is finally going to take the leap into matrimony. Lesser men have crumbled and caved before him, but Ned stood tall. Until now. We're all sorry you're giving up the ghost, Ned, but happy to welcome you to the ranks of married men. Good luck, pal!"

Rosebud crossed her arms over her camisole. Hardly a ringing endorsement. And she didn't care for that "giving up the ghost" bit, either.

"Waiter, more wine," Vanessa called out, while everyone else was still toasting. The waiter scurried to bring another bottle, while she sniffed, "The service here is horrible."

Really, Rosebud didn't have to try to make Vanessa

look awful. Sulky, scrawny, unpleasant, dry as toast, the woman was very good at looking bad all by herself!

Vanessa's empty wineglass gave her an idea. If Vanessa kept drinking at the rate she was going, after shoving all of her food aside, she might start behaving even worse. So far, all she'd done was act like a snob. But if she got sloppy or weepy or danced on the table, it would be even more embarrassing. Surely Ned wouldn't marry a common tosspot.

So she whipped into the catering kitchen and down to the wine cellar, pilfered some champagne and a very nice merlot and some lovely dessert wines to add to the carts, and kept sticking more bottles in front of the waiters every time they turned around. The liquor began to flow.

Back in the dining room, Rosebud noticed that everyone was getting a little sloshed, but she hovered around Vanessa. "More champagne," she whispered in her ear. "Drink up."

"Oooh, good idea," someone exclaimed behind her.

Rosebud spun around as the flickering image of a fellow ghost appeared at her shoulder. "Mimi? I thought you were busy with the bride who didn't want to come out of the bathroom."

"*Zut alors!* I thought she would nevair leave!" Mimi threw up her hands, accidentally slugging Rosebud with one of the wide sleeves of the Parisian robe she was so proud of. "*Mais oui*, now she has consented to come out. My technique was the very same as you. I feed her champagne. *Une* glass, *deux* glass, *trois*. Voilà! *L'amour!*"

"Congratulations," Rosebud offered. Jolly for Mimi

to have conquered her recalcitrant bride problem. But that still didn't explain why she was hanging around here. "Shouldn't you be collecting your gold star or something?"

"Mademoiselle Arlotta, she asked me to come and oversee, yes? 'Poor Rosebud,' she says, 'she is hopeless.'" Mimi shrugged. "But I see now you are fine. You ply your bride with liqueur, and all is well. I shall report zis to Mademoiselle Arlotta."

"You do that," Rosebud returned, happy to note that Mimi had vanished into thin air. Under her breath, she muttered, "Drat. I didn't mean to use a technique that actually *worked.* No more liquor for you, missy."

To distract Vanessa from her wineglass, Rosebud tried one of her favorite tricks. She was very fond of electronics, and Vanessa's tiny phone was really cute. It took practically nothing to give it a quick zap and make it ring.

But when Vanessa reached into her bag to answer her phone, it stopped ringing. As she stared at the phone, quite confused, Ned's mother sent her another disapproving glance.

"Maybe you should turn it off, Vanessa," her future mother-in-law offered. Rosebud only smiled.

And as soon as Vanessa put the phone away, Rosebud rang it again. And a third time, just for kicks.

"I do not understand this," Vanessa said angrily. Raising her voice, she demanded, "Is someone at this table calling me and hanging up before I answer? Lauren, is this your idea of a practical joke?" She sent her sister a withering glare, but the matron of honor raised her hands to show that she had no phone, that she was completely innocent.

"Don't worry about it, Van," her father said gruffly. "Put the phone away and turn it off. This isn't the time."

"Excellent advice," Mrs. Mulgrew agreed dryly.

Ned backed up his mother, bless his heart. "Really, Van, you don't need the phone now."

"I guess I'm outnumbered." Switching the phone off with a jab, she slid it into her red purse and then set the purse on the table next to her plate. Rosebud took that opportunity to knock all Vanessa's silverware onto the floor. It was that sort of minor irritation she'd planned at the beginning, before she got sidetracked by Ned.

"Fat lot of good that did me," Rosebud whispered.

"How did you do that?" Vanessa's mother inquired, crawling under the table to retrieve the fork and spoon. "Van, how did you manage to knock all your silver off the table? How much have you had to drink?"

"Mother, leave it. The waiter will take care of it." Vanessa waved a careless hand. "I don't know how I did. In fact, I don't think I *did* do it. I couldn't possibly have knocked my silverware on the floor." She scanned the area for someone to blame, but there was nobody there.

While they were all busy rounding up her silverware, Rosebud slid the whole purse off the table and hid it under Grandmother Westicott's chair.

"My purse is missing!" Vanessa cried. "Who took my purse?"

"I'm sure no one stole your purse," Ned's dad tried.

Even he, Vanessa's biggest fan, looked less than amused by the brouhaha she was creating.

"I want to know where my purse is. It was right here a minute ago and now it's gone." Vanessa stalked to the other table, jabbing a finger at her sister. "Lauren, stand up and back away from your chair. I know you've got it."

"Vanessa, I didn't take your purse!" Lauren protested. Her husband chimed in that he could verify she hadn't left her seat.

"You've always been so jealous of me, Lauren. You're trying to make me look bad, aren't you? Calling my phone and stealing my purse. How childish!"

Her sister slapped her napkin down on the table as she jumped to her feet. "Who's the jealous one, Vanessa? I already have the husband and kids you're dying for. And I'm younger!"

Vanessa crossed her thin arms over her scarlet dress, shouting, "I should never have asked you to be in my wedding party. I should've known you'd find a way to ruin everything."

"Me? Me? I didn't even want to be your matron of honor. You picked a dress that looks hideous on me. On purpose!"

"Well, I didn't want you, either!"

"Ned, maybe you should, you know, take Vanessa outside or something. Talk to her. Calm her down," his father suggested quietly as the sisters continued to hurl insults at each other.

"Yeah, you're right." Ned rose, squaring his jaw, intent on doing his duty.

As for her, Rosebud backed away from the whole

melee. Who knew all that would happen from a few innocent tricks? Yes, it was mostly Rosebud's fault, and maybe it was because the liquor had loosened their tongues, but Vanessa had jumped to the conclusion the culprit was her sister all by herself. Who could've predicted that? Rosebud had only intended to provoke her, make a little mischief, not turn her into Lizzie Borden.

Watching the family squabble, seeing the embarrassment on the faces of all the guests and relatives who were witnessing it, Rosebud began to feel pretty ashamed of herself. Quickly she slipped the red leather bag onto Vanessa's chair while the sisters continued to bicker.

"Van," Ned cut in, taking her hand, trying to pull her away, "sweetheart, listen to me. Lauren didn't do anything. With the phone, I'm sure it was just some kind of malfunction. We're up in the mountains and this is an old hotel. There are probably all kinds of weird signals."

"And what about my purse?" Vanessa shot back.

In a soothing tone, he said, "Why don't we look for it? It probably fell under the table."

Rosebud gave the chair leg a tiny kick to bring it to someone's attention.

"Actually," Vanessa's mother offered, looking quite shell-shocked, "it's right on your chair, Van."

"On my chair?" Vanessa's narrow eyebrows shot so high they almost flew off her head entirely. "How did it get on my chair?"

"Don't you think you left it there?" Ned asked innocently.

"No," his fiancée snapped. "I do not think I left it there. Someone here is trying to drive me insane, that's all!"

Poor Ned. He asked, "Why would anyone do that?"

The question just hung there in the air, awkward and unanswerable.

"Van, we need to talk," he said softly. "Why don't we let everyone here finish their dessert, and we'll take a walk, calm down and sort things out. Okay?"

He set an arm around his fiancée's shoulder, steering her toward the door. The faces in that room were so serious it looked more like a wake than a wedding.

On one hand, Rosebud was still suffering from guilt, that she had created such a to-do.

On the other... When Ned said *We need to talk*, it sounded to her like *I need to break it off*. She distinctly remembered someone saying in a movie that *We need to talk* was a very bad thing to hear.

Could Ned really be on the verge of calling off the wedding? Could her plan really have succeeded, as mixed-up and haphazard as it had been?

She squinted at Ned, trying to gauge his expression. As he pulled Vanessa aside, Rosebud rushed over there, anxious to keep close enough to hear every word.

Unfortunately she was so anxious not to get left behind that she didn't pay attention to what she was doing. As she rushed, she created a big whoosh of cold air that billowed behind them at the same time Ned and Vanessa reached the door.

Vanessa shivered, Ned halted in midstep, wheeling to glance over his shoulder, and an oncoming waiter carrying a laden tray tripped over the tip of Ned's shoe. Rosebud watched, horrified, as an open bottle of dessert wine rocketed off the tray, splashing dark red wine all over Vanessa and her scarlet dress, from the top of her head to the tips of her pointy red stilettos.

There was utter silence in the room. It was so quiet Rosebud actually heard the drip, drip, drip of wine off Vanessa's nose.

And then everybody started talking at once, somebody loudly calling for a towel and somebody else for seltzer, while the hapless waiter kept apologizing and trying to dab at Vanessa with a napkin. Not much was coming out of her. Sort of a whimper. Ned kept his arm securely around his bride-to-be, oblivious to how wet she was, assuring everyone that she was fine and they were fine and they were going to call it a night, thanks.

Still stunned, Rosebud wasn't sure what to do. The best policy seemed to be retreat. Careful not to create any more updrafts, she slunk off to a corner where she couldn't get into any more trouble.

As Ned bundled Vanessa off, the people left behind looked at each other and quietly departed, too, not really saying anything to each other. It was as if they'd all survived a train wreck, and they just wanted to get off the train before the next crash. They'd probably dine out on this for months, but for today... The general consensus seemed to be that this was a pot best left unstirred.

The last guests in the room were Ned's aunt and uncle, who'd been trying to fade into the woodwork over in the corner, not far from Rosebud.

"Well, that was the most memorable rehearsal dinner I've ever seen," announced Uncle Jerry.

"You said it," his wife agreed. She shook her head. "I would love to get Ned's girlfriend into therapy, I'll tell you that."

"You know, hon, I never try to second-guess what people see in each other," he said slowly. "But I just don't get why Ned is taking on that kind of drama. Ned has always been so smart, so steady. Why would he marry someone who loses it over the little stuff?"

Above his head, Rosebud sent down the mental message, *I don't understand it, either, Uncle Jerry!*

Aunt Win lifted her shoulders in a shrug. "Maybe she's just coming unglued because of the wedding. It happens. But it makes you wonder what she's going to be like when the marriage hits its first snag. Those weren't exactly major problems happening here."

"Exactly my point. If you fall apart over little stuff, what's going to happen when you hit the big ones?"

"Maybe there's more going on than we know about," she suggested. "It's just... This is lousy. Ned is such a great guy. I adore him. Totally my favorite nephew. He should marry the best woman ever."

Jerry patted her arm fondly. "Sometimes I've felt like he was more our kid than Jack and Lisa's."

"I know." She frowned. "I like Lisa, but... That marriage is so sterile you could do surgery on it. I guess that's where Ned is taking his cues from. Marriage as a business deal, you know?"

"You think so?" Jerry put his arm around his wife and gave her a squeeze. "I kind of hoped he'd use us as his model."

"Yeah, well, that's not happening," she said slowly. "When he told us he was finally getting married, I thought it had to be for love. Then I thought it was because she had money. Now I'm starting to wonder if it's some white knight thing, like he thinks he can save her."

"A better idea," her husband noted, "would be to save himself."

Hear, hear.

"You mean call it off? Do you really think the Ned we know is capable of calling off a wedding at the last minute? You said it—he's never been one for drama," Win mused. "Plus there's the lawyer thing. He's always prided himself on being so ethical and reliable."

"He'll do what he needs to do," Ned's uncle replied cryptically, leading his wife out of the dining room.

Rosebud wished she knew what that meant. After all this, she had high hopes that Ned would at least emerge with a clearer head and one less fiancée. Fingers crossed.

She lifted her chin. "If that happens, even if I never see him again, it was worth it. I saved him."

As for her... Saving herself was going to be a trickier proposition. Even if Miss Arlotta hadn't witnessed any of this firsthand, somebody was bound to say something. And who knew what kind of punishment Miss A and the Judge would come up with?

With that thought in mind, Rosebud shot out of the dining room like a cannon, headed for her hideaway in the attic. She knew her hour of reckoning was coming. Fast.

Miss Arlotta was going to have her head on a platter for this escapade.

5

"ROSEBUD?" Miss Arlotta's voice got louder, echoing into every corner of the attic. "Rosebud? My chambers. Now."

Here it was. The summons she'd been dreading.

Alone in her secret alcove, Rosebud started to get ready. She knew she couldn't hide out too long, especially if Miss A was already mad at her. If she had to show up, she might as well go prepared.

She concentrated, sucking all the color out of her skin, turning herself as pale and ashen as possible. She thought she normally looked quite healthy for a ghost, but better to go with "death warmed over" right now. So she rubbed her eyes for that red, hollow look, raked her hands through her curls to send them into disarray, untied a ribbon or two, put a streak of dust on her face and practiced generating a tiny tear to trickle down her cheek. She was going to need all the sympathy she could muster.

Letting her head droop, doing her best to look tragic, she slipped over to the main part of the attic to present herself before the boss. She fully expected Miss A to see through her Poor Pitiful Me charade immediately, but maybe Judge Hangen, Miss Arlotta's beau, would be more gullible and toss a little mercy her way.

She hazarded a glance up under her lashes. What?

No judge. No jury of her peers. Just the boss behind her huge carved mahogany desk, and a few of the girls lounging elsewhere in the room. Glory was helping Mimi apply polish to her toenails while Lavender took a nap on a chaise. How very odd.

"Did you call for me, Miss Arlotta?" Rosebud inquired cautiously.

"I sure as heck did," the madam replied. She lifted a hand in a grand gesture, and out of nowhere, the imposing volume known as the Bedpost Book appeared. Miss Arlotta licked her index finger as she perused a page.

Rosebud closed her eyes. How bad was it going to be? She already had so many black marks in the Bedpost Book. What difference would a few more make? And without the judge and the jury, her punishment couldn't be too horrific, could it? *Oh, yes, it could.* She had no idea how far Miss A's powers extended.

She braced herself for bad news.

Miss Arlotta looked up from the book. "I'm as surprised as you are, but you're here for a gold star, darlin'."

"I—I'm what?" She staggered backward. "Gold star?"

"I had Mimi keepin' an eye on your assignment. She told me about how you pulled the old melt-her-with-liquor trick on your bride." The madam shook her lemonade-colored curls. "That gambit's got hair on it, it's so old. Not what you might call inspired but, heck, if it works, I ain't complainin'."

Rosebud retreated even farther from the desk and Miss Arlotta's all-seeing gaze. Shielding her eyes with one hand, she mulled this over. She still wasn't exactly sure what was happening here. Gold stars were not all that familiar to her. Was it possible to offer a commendation like that, and then lower the boom by taking it away and inflicting dire punishment right after?

Or could Miss Arlotta be a bit behind in her newsgathering, what with how busy the hotel and the ghostly honeymoon helpers had been recently, and not aware yet of what had transpired?

"So this is all because I plied my bride with liquor?" she asked slowly.

"Well, no. Not just that. You wouldn't be getting that gold star just for getting a girl drunk." Miss A planted her hands on her broad hips. "No, you wouldn't."

"No?"

"Not a chance." Now she leaned over the desk, fixing Rosebud with a meaningful stare.

Uh-oh. This didn't look good. Rosebud envisioned the gold star ripped away as Miss Arlotta's ire and a flurry of black marks rained down on her head.

"I was busy with some other things and you're always kind of a gray area for me to read, so I won't kid you," the madam continued. "I don't exactly have every last detail of how you did it. But I do know you managed to thaw the chill amongst your betrothed couple."

"I did?"

Miss Arlotta grinned. "You surely did, hon. You got your bride bollixed up enough that your groom got to jump in and act manly on her behalf and strip 'er down to 'er altogethers."

He did *what?* Just because the twit had a little wine

splashed on her, Ned leaped into *undressing* her? As she felt her temper start to simmer, Rosebud clenched her hands into fists.

"Now that, hon, is just the kind of gumption I like to see." Looking very pleased, the madam began to pace behind the massive desk, swishing her bustle from side to side with authority. "Yessiree. That's what I call taking the reins and runnin' with 'em. Why, after you dumped all that wine on the bride, the boy got entrée right into the suite she'd heretofore denied him."

"He did?"

"Sure did. And what with her all wet and him helping undress 'er and clean 'er up, with the bubbles and the lather and a whole lot of slippery, naked flesh..." She smiled fondly. "I'll bet those two are going at it hot as all get out right about now."

Rosebud pressed her eyes shut. Ned and Vanessa sloshing in bubbles, soaping up wet, naked flesh... Those were mental images she didn't need to see. Ever.

Miss Arlotta didn't seem to notice her distress, rattling on with relish. "Always a good idea to concoct some way for somebody to lose the better part of their clothes. I need to write that down to tell all the girls. Once you get their clothes off 'em, the job's a durn sight easier."

I didn't mean to get her clothes off! Rosebud protested silently.

"Mimi, you listenin'? You make a note of that," Miss A instructed. "Let everybody know they can do themselves a favor if they get 'em wet or dirty or ripped or something. Heck, whip off their clothes in a tornado. But get 'em down to the skin, by hook or by crook."

"Ah, *oui.* So romantic."

"I got a thing for bathin' myself," Glory put in dreamily from the side. "I don't know why, but I do. If you get your folks good and dirty and they can bathe each other, I don't know about y'all, but it sure seems romantical to me if the boy starts shampooing her hair and the like."

"I never thought about it," Rosebud said flatly. Hair-washing wasn't high on her list of romantic activities.

Especially not if it was Ned, washing wine out of Vanessa's hair while she moaned, *Ooooh, oooh, Ned, right there, that spot.* Talk about disgusting.

Feeling weak and more than a tad nauseated, she put her hand over her mouth. Still...

She narrowed her eyes. Had someone verified this whole scenario or was it just supposition at this point? Had anyone actually dropped into the Lady Godiva Suite to check on Ned and Vanessa and witnessed all this horrifying bathing behavior? She'd thought for certain Ned and Vanessa were headed for a breakup when they left the dining room.

Could it really have turned to passion so easily once they got upstairs, all because Rosebud had accidentally triggered a major wine spill and some clothing got removed?

Miss Arlotta beamed at Rosebud, looking proud enough to bust her buttons. "You know, hon," the boss declared, "I am right proud that you have seen fit to try to improve your attitude and get your couple on the road to bedroom bliss. I was starting to despair of you ever comin' around, Rosebud, and I frankly did not believe you when you said you only kissed him to get him stoked up. I thought you was lying for sure. But you have done real good work here under trying circumstances. Real good."

"Thank you, Miss Arlotta," she said miserably.

"You are very welcome." She went back to the Bedpost Book, adopting a more formal tone. "In light of how you, firstly, maneuvered 'em both into the same suite when they was previously separate, and secondly, as a result of your actions got 'em naked as jaybirds and well on the path to bedroom bliss two days ahead of deadline, Rosebud, my dear, I am happy to inform you that you have been awarded one gold star for meritorious service."

Jolly.

"Go on, Rosebud," Glory whispered. "Go on and tell her you're grateful. Maybe she'll throw in another gold star."

But she had more important things than that silly Bedpost Book on her mind. "While I really appreciate your kindness, Miss A, and I do hope you'll forgive me if I'm being overzealous, I feel the need to verify that all this passion you're talking about actually happened."

"I got a lot more experience with this kind of thing than you do," the boss reminded her. "I know what adds up to what."

Rosebud remained unconvinced.

"All right then, Mimi, you tell her. You saw the boy undress his bride, didn't you?"

"Ah, *oui*, yes, I did. Mademoiselle Arlotta sends me down to zee and I zee. Wiz my own eyes. I see him unzeep ze scarlet dress of ze girl, yes?" Mimi smiled. "Zis girl, she is a beeg mess. Zo, she isn't wearing much, he takes off what she is, she shivers, he tell her, now we take a leetle bath. Voilà!" She shrugged. "I leave them alone to enjoy ze bath."

Rosebud's heart lodged in her throat.

"It don't take a hooker to know what comes next," Miss Arlotta noted dryly.

"But..." Carefully, trying not to show how upset she was at the very idea of Ned and Vanessa and their "leetle bath," she argued, "I just want to be sure I deserve that gold star. I don't want anything I don't deserve."

"This being only your second gold star and all, I can't fault you for wanting things done right. So you go ahead and verify if you feel the need," the madam proclaimed. "But then give the kids some privacy, you hear? Now that you turned up the heat on 'em, they can keep the fire stoked all by themselves from here on in."

Rosebud's voice was very small when she responded, "Yes, ma'am."

"All right then, you hop into the Lady Godiva Suite and give 'em a look-see. But then you take the rest of the night off. You deserve it. You got a gold star, hon. You're on your way." It was clear she was trying to sound positive and supportive, but Miss Arlotta's gaze was shrewd. "You can pick 'em up again tomorrow if you think they need another push."

Rosebud was out of there in a flash, determined to get out from under Miss A's scrutiny. Besides, she had to know the truth.

Were they headed toward a breakup, as she'd surmised when they left the dining room? Or a hot-blooded make-up, as Mimi and Miss Arlotta seemed to think? Which would it be for Ned and Vanessa?

Once she was there, Rosebud hesitated outside the door to the Lady Godiva Suite. It had seemed like a good idea to make sure what was going on, but... If they really were in the midst of a mating dance and she witnessed it, would she ever recover?

"They aren't," she said stubbornly. "Ned doesn't love her. He isn't in love with her. He wouldn't. He might've helped her take off her dress and even run her a bath, but that is it."

She began to step through the wall. But she pulled back.

If nothing happened, why had Mimi thought there was so much more? Why had Miss Arlotta awarded her the gold star? And what was all that nonsense about the bathing and the bubbles?

She pressed her hands over her temples, trying to squash out all the bad thoughts.

"I don't believe he made love to her tonight."

But what if he did? Or what if he were making love to her right now, right inside the Lady Godiva Suite? If she went in there, would she trip over those two bodies entwined, rolling around in mindless passion?

"I can always drop a sofa on them," she said darkly. "Or maybe two."

Taking a deep breath, Rosebud held her head high as she slipped through the wall into the suite.

NED HELPED VANESSA into the shower and then he retreated to the living room. What a god-awful mess.

With his fiancée and his life cracking into bits around him, getting her out of the line of fire, out of the wine-soaked dress and into the shower seemed like the least he could do. But what now?

After pacing around the living room of the suite, he took a seat and dropped his head into his hands. Poor Vanessa. No wonder she was going crazy. She prided herself on perfection, but her rehearsal dinner had been anything but. And her parents and his parents and her sister, the one he had just discovered she was insanely jealous of, had all witnessed the meltdown.

"I need a drink," he said out loud. "A stiff drink."

Which raised another issue. Just how much had his fiancée had to drink tonight? He'd never seen her behave like this before. Could it be a booze issue? Was this something he was going to have to watch out for?

"I don't think I like being an adult." He stood up again and ran a hand through his hair. He felt as if he were crossing a minefield. Relationships, marriage, maturity, responsibility... Maybe he wasn't as ready as he'd thought.

He heard the shower stop running, and after a moment Vanessa emerged, her hair hanging, still wet, over the shoulders of the thick white hotel bathrobe she'd wrapped herself in. The thing dragged along the floor and went well past her hands. Looking very small and unsure of herself, she sat in a hot-pink chair opposite him.

Small and unsure... That was not how he thought of Vanessa.

Leaning forward from his own chair, Ned took her

hands in his. "Van, I'm sorry for the way the dinner turned out. I know you wanted it to be perfect."

"It wasn't my fault," she said quickly. "I went over the details with those people a hundred times. And I still don't know what was going on with my phone and my purse and my silverware... How can I be expected to cope with that kind of irritation?"

"Don't think about it anymore, okay? It's over. You said yourself we didn't need a rehearsal, so who cares what the rehearsal dinner turned out to be?"

"I care!"

Ned leaned back. "Listen, Van, let it go, okay? I don't think either of us has been acting like ourselves lately. I've been distracted..." *And obsessed with a chambermaid I met for three minutes.* He shook that off. Not the right time to go there. If only his thoughts would stop returning like some kind of homing pigeon, right back to Rose, every time he breathed. "I know I haven't been as involved as I could've been while you were planning all this."

"That's an understatement," she snapped, shoving her hands into the pockets of her robe.

"You haven't been acting normal, either," he reminded her.

"Great." She focused on the ceiling. "First my rehearsal dinner is a fiasco, and now my fiancé is raking me over the coals. Just what I need."

"I'm not raking you over the coals," he told her. "I'm just saying that all the time we were dating, you were so calm, so secure, so easy to be with. And you haven't been that way since...well, since I proposed."

"Now I'm some shrew, is that what you're saying?"

"Of course not." Although she was getting close, he had to admit.

Vanessa pushed back, rising and pacing behind her chair. "I've been under a lot of stress. You don't know what it's like to put a whole wedding together—the kind you and I deserve—in a month. It's insane."

"I understand that. But you're the one who said we had to do it in August." He never had understood the rush. In fact, that was part of what had made him start to question her and him and the two of them together. If the only way to get married was to run headlong into it without stopping to breathe, was it really the right thing?

"I wanted to do it now. I've been waiting so long," she argued. "Ned, I am thirty-one years old. My sister got married at twenty-five. My mother got married at twenty-one. All of my friends from college are married. They're settled, with babies and nannies and families. I'm thirty-one! I have nothing!"

He tried to be soothing. "Whether we get married or not, that's not true."

"Whether or not? Are you saying *not* is an option?" she shouted. "Because it isn't. We *are* getting married. Friday. We are!"

Ned stood up and crossed to her, putting his hands on her arms. "Calm down, Vanessa. Don't do this."

"Look at me," she cried, circling in front of him. "I'm pulled together, I'm thin, I'm beautiful, I have money, I am on a thousand committees and I know people. I get things done. I'm fabulous, damn it! Why am I not married?"

Ned found her words utterly appalling, but she

seemed to be waiting for some kind of response from him. He figured he was on shaky ground whatever he said. How had he gotten himself into this? *You asked her to marry you, you idiot.*

"Van, I think you're asking all the wrong questions," he tried. "Instead of 'Why am I not married?' maybe you should be working on 'Why am I getting married *now,* to this person?' Because it isn't fair to you or me if this is just some footrace we're running, if we're crossing the finish line because everybody else already has and we don't want to be left behind."

Vanessa pressed her lips together until they disappeared. He could tell she was furious. "Is that what you think?"

Honestly, for him... Yes, that *was* what he thought. It was a relief to realize that. There he was, back on July Fourth. He'd looked at himself in the mirror and decided he needed to be settled. He'd thought, hell, I'm thirty, time to fish or cut bait. He'd been dating Vanessa for two years, he liked her fine, he'd never met anyone else who flipped his switches, so why not? She'd seemed thrilled, eager to become his wife. She was a perfect choice. His father said so, his friends thought so...

How was he supposed to know he'd end up, one short month later, more confused and unhappy than he'd ever been, while she turned into a raging head-case he couldn't even like, let alone love? But, of course, he couldn't tell her that. Any of it.

"I don't know what I think," he said instead.

But he did know. It was clear now that he'd decided to marry Vanessa for all the wrong reasons. At the top of the list, because he was tired of being alone and he didn't think he would ever meet anyone better. Cynical, rational Ned Mulgrew. He was a lawyer. The firm was full of divorce cases. He didn't believe in love or romance. It had never touched him yet—why should he believe in it?

Because, now, just to really put the icing on his crumbling mental cake, he *had* met someone better. He'd met Rose.

Ned turned away from his fiancée. This was absurd. He was probably just grasping at straws. She couldn't possibly be as beautiful and bright and captivating as she seemed.

But why couldn't he find her again?

"God, what a mess," he muttered.

"What does that mean?" Vanessa's voice took on an edge of hysteria. "We are not calling off this wedding, Ned. Don't even think of it. I will not be humiliated in front of my friends and family because you've decided you don't want to grow up."

"That's not what it's about."

"Sure it is." Vanessa shook her head hard enough to splatter him with water drops from her wet hair. "You're not ready to grow up and join the adult world and get married. That's why you took two years to propose, because you were playing Peter Pan games."

"That's not fair—"

She advanced on him, adopting a more pleading tone, grabbing for his hands. "Look, Ned, we're good together. I know these past few weeks have been rough, but we can make it. We can. Just hang on, okay? Everybody starts to panic when they think about signing away the rest of their lives. It's normal. So we're both panicking and acting crazy. Once we're married, it will be fine. You'll see."

He might be a total idiot, he might even be the biggest jerk in Colorado, but even he couldn't look her in the eye and tell her the wedding was off. Maybe she was right. Maybe everyone felt this way and it was completely normal.

"Sleep on it, Neddy," she said sweetly. She stretched up to give him a kiss, and he couldn't help but notice that it felt cold and wet, and it left him completely unaffected. One kiss from a burglar and he was smitten. Hundreds of kisses from the woman he was supposed to marry, and he didn't feel a thing.

He backed away.

Vanessa smiled, blowing him another kiss. "Sleep on it," she repeated. "We'll forget about the ghastly rehearsal dinner, I'll see you tomorrow, and everything will be better then."

He didn't say anything, just turned on his heel and left the Lady Godiva Suite, anxious to get back to his room and think about things. His mind was a jumble of conflicting thoughts. Vanessa, Rose, what his future held...

Would anything be better tomorrow? "Don't count on it," he said under his breath.

But he stopped right there in the middle of the hallway. He could've sworn there was a warm glow wrapped around him where he stood. The temperature in the hallway had been perfectly normal till then, but now...warm and toasty. As if he were standing in a pool of warm sunshine.

It was kind of the way he'd felt when he was at the rehearsal dinner, when he'd been gloomy and mixed up, and then suddenly his gaze had been pulled to the empty air behind his uncle. His mother had freaked out and called him on it, wanting to know what he was doing. He'd had no explanation. But he'd felt happy sitting there, staring and smiling into space, as if some invisible, positive force had been suspended there, wrapping joy around him.

"Oh, Lord, now I'm definitely losing it. This isn't *Star Trek*. There aren't force fields of happiness popping up around me."

He glanced around the hallway. Maybe the heating was uneven in this old building. He felt sure that must be it. He was getting a blast from some register or heating coil he just couldn't see.

But why had his mood improved as soon as he stepped into the hot spot?

"Okay, never mind. I'm tired, I'm confused, I've had more drama in two days than the rest of my life combined, and I'm letting the crazy bordello atmosphere in this hotel get to me." He marched himself down the hall, he pounded up the stairs and let himself into his room, slamming the door behind him.

No burglars tonight. No Rose. No funky warm glow in the room, either. He prowled around the whole place, looking under the bed and in the shower stall, even in the armoire. But there were no strange hot spots. Just an empty room.

Exhausted, Ned peeled off his clothes and climbed into bed naked. He didn't care if his jacket or his pants got wrinkled on the floor all night.

"I need sleep," he said out loud. Punching his pillow, he turned over, knocked some of his covers off, and closed his eyes. "Sleep."

SHE WASN'T SUPPOSED to be there. This was so wrong there wasn't even a rule for it.

But once again, Rosebud couldn't help herself. She'd been so overjoyed to find him talking to Vanessa—just talking, no bare skin, no flailing limbs, no hanky-panky whatsoever—that she'd wrapped herself around him in the hallway in an otherworldly hug. And then when he'd sort of overreacted, she'd backed off, giving him some space and time to do whatever it was he needed to do.

Except... Alone in her hideaway, tucked into the attic, she'd found herself wondering what he was doing and whether he was okay. Before she knew it, there she was, floating into his room, taking a peek. Too bad she got there after he'd stripped off all his clothes. She was really, really sorry she'd missed that.

But now, here she was, perched on the polished wood of his curved headboard, watching him sleep. He lay on his side, and his beautiful face was pressed into the pillow, his lashes dark and lush against his cheek.

"Such a gorgeous man," she whispered, dipping closer, allowing herself to brush a finger over his soft cheek.

The rest of him looked pretty tasty as well, with one bare arm and leg tossed over the bedclothes. The hard muscles in his arm and thigh, the smooth curve of his bottom, the way his skin glowed golden in the moonlight that seeped in through the lace curtains.... He was irresistible.

Poor Ned. Adorable. Irresistible. And so unhappy, sleeping in that bed alone, baffled and bewildered about what he wanted from his life.

"He needs me," she murmured. Was she trying to convince herself? Or establishing a case for later, if she got caught?

"Oh, fiddlesticks! I'm not hurting anyone," she scoffed.

Before she changed her mind, she removed her spectacles and set them on the windowsill. Then she moved back to the bed, easing herself in, sliding into the small empty space behind him.

"After all, Miss Arlotta herself said I deserved the night off," she reasoned. "Miss A thinks he's safely romping with the odious Vanessa. And she thinks *I'm* safely tucked away all by myself till morning. Therefore no one is paying any attention to either of us. Which leaves me free to devote my entire night to my beloved Ned."

Ooops. She sat up in the bed. Since when was Ned her *beloved* instead of simply her assignment?

Beloved? Rosebud wasn't sure she'd ever felt this strange, warm cozy glow spreading through her body, starting deep within. It made her want to wrap herself around Ned and never let go.

"I do love him," she said out loud. How utterly astonishing. She loved Ned Mulgrew.

It was wonderful.

Rosebud felt taller, lighter, better all around. She

loved him! It was the most magical thing she'd ever encountered.

Right now, she planned to lie down beside him, listen to him breathe, press close to his heartbeat and hold him in her arms all night long. She would think about the complications tomorrow.

"He'll never know," she whispered as she snuggled into the bed, fitting her breasts against his back, her thighs against his bottom. She sighed. A perfect fit.

Making herself three-dimensional for a brief moment, she gazed down at the sight of her arm, pale and slender, across his strong, tawny flesh, at how possessive her hand looked where it lay against his bare hipbone.

"I'm not going to touch anything I'm not supposed to," she promised. "My hand will go no farther than the hipbone. No matter how tempting it is."

Because this was amazing. She realized that although she'd shared her body with Edmund, she'd never spent a whole night with him. She'd never *slept* with him. And now she was glad. The first man she actually slept with got to be Ned.

Closing her eyes, Rosebud let herself fade back to invisibility as she wrapped herself around Ned. Dropping off to sleep, she murmured, "I'll leave before he wakes up. No one will ever be the wiser."

6

Thursday morning

ROSEBUD AWOKE to the wonderful feeling of someone breathing on the back of her neck. Drowsy, safe, sheltered, she smiled into the pillow. There was an arm around her waist, a strong, warm arm, and her backside was nestled right up against someone else's front side. Someone's naked, hard, intriguing, blazing hot, extremely *masculine* front side.

Ned. Her eyes shot open. *Oh, no.* She was in Ned's bed! With Ned. Naked! She ran a shaky hand down his muscular thigh to be sure. Oh, he was naked, all right.

Snatching her hand back before she ventured into even more frightening territory, she held herself perfectly motionless, but it didn't help. He was still breathing on her. And she could still feel the tantalizing pressure of what she thought must be his erect manhood pressing into the back of her thin cotton drawers. All she had to do was turn around...

It was torture, agony and heaven, all rolled into one terrifying package.

"I think I'm in trouble," she whispered, trying to come up with some sort of plan.

How did she get into this fix? She wasn't supposed to sleep this long. Ghosts didn't sleep this long! She certainly wasn't supposed to be here when he woke up.

That was an even worse thought. Had he woken up? She glanced over her shoulder. His eyes were closed, and the rhythmic in and out that she could feel throughout her body every time he breathed told her he was still asleep. Disaster averted. But for how long? Could she possibly get herself out of here before he opened his eyes or figured out that there was a warm body—a warm *invisible* body—lying between him and the wall?

She was good and stuck where she was. His arm was clamped around her, holding her fast, although she hadn't really expected it to work that way. Technically, shouldn't his arm have slipped right through her invisible body?

"I don't know," she said under her breath, trying to ease herself out from under him but getting nowhere. "I never slept with anybody while I was invisible before!"

Now that she thought about it, she also had no idea how she'd gotten here. She felt quite sure she'd started out on the other side, behind him, next to the edge of the bed, ready for an easy exit. But now, squashed between him and the wall, she was trapped.

"Mmmph," he mumbled in her ear, rustling around a little. And then he dipped his head, rubbed his cheek on her arm at precisely the place where her strap had slipped off her shoulder, and made an "Mmm..." noise.

Rosebud stiffened. That had a different ring to it. It was more like how she sounded when she licked the frosting off chocolate cake. Coming from Ned at this particular moment, it sounded dangerous. Like he was enjoying the feel of her next to him. Like he was eager for more.

And like he was waking up.

Closing her eyes, she concentrated and hastily flashed her body into full-color 3-D form. It was the only thing she could think of. If he was fully conscious, it had to be better for him to find a whole girl in bed with him than a transparent mass of energy particles.

"Mmm-hmm," he said again, more forcefully this time, as he moved his hand up to squeeze her breast above the line of her corset.

Rosebud gasped with surprise and the pure, intense pleasure of it. She couldn't breathe—her corset was suddenly much too tight, and her breasts were very close to spilling out over the lacy edge of her camisole—and she felt shaky and strange, as if her skin were on fire. Maybe she'd just forgotten what skin felt like. Was it supposed to be this sensitive? Was she supposed to be trembling and quivering, dizzy and woozy, begging for more?

She wished she'd thought to get out of these clothes or conjure up a different outfit before she materialized. Changing her ghostly attire was tricky business that took extra effort, though, and she hadn't had time. Sure she could get out of these, but she had to create replacements out of thin air. Plus she wasn't exactly sure it would work. But the lace of her camisole was itchy against her breasts and the knickers were scrunched up around her legs. And damn that corset. She couldn't seem to take in enough air.

Still, his hands felt so good. Her body was blooming under his caress, melting, responding in ways she didn't know it could. As his fingers tweaked her nipple, it peaked and hardened under the lace, and she found herself curling into him, letting him explore whatever he wanted to. It felt too good and it had been too long since she'd been touched. Way too long.

Just a few minutes, she told herself. *He'll wake up, or he'll move and I can escape. But right now... Right now... Just a little more...*

His lips grazed the nape of her neck. "So soft," he murmured, gently moving her hair aside, tracing the line of her shoulder with his kisses, nudging the light chemise out of his way.

She knew he had to be at least partly awake to negotiate her clothing that well, but she didn't care. She shifted around in his arms so that she could face him. So that she could kiss him.

His mouth slanted over hers, hungry and demanding, and she gave him back exactly what he asked for. The kiss was hot and deep. Dark. Unrelenting. It was as if he were trying to imprint the taste of her kiss into his memory. And she wanted that, too.

But Rosebud knew, even if she was stuck at the Inn for another 109 years, she would never forget his kiss. As his tongue tangled with hers, she found herself making greedy little moans, pushing up into him, telegraphing that she wanted more.

Ned bracketed her face with his hands, holding her steady for that unbelievable kiss, but then he slid his hands to her bodice, pushing the scratchy lace out of his way and freeing her breasts completely. It was intoxicating and overwhelming and maddening, all at the same time. As she pitched backward into the soft bed, she wondered how it was possible to feel so many things.

Her body rocked with sensation after sensation. With his mouth on hers, one hand firmly on her breast, the other roaming down her hip and around the edge of her bloomers, teasing the inside of her thigh... She couldn't do anything but open the floodgates and *feel*.

No wonder all the other girls were so anxious to seduce a groom here or there. Was it always like this? No, it couldn't be. This was different. Unique. All about Ned. And about her. About how perfectly they fit together. About the fierce, insistent throb of passion between them.

She wanted to be naked under him. Now. Before either of them came to their senses. But there were too many strings and ribbons and hooks. And her hands were shaking as she tried to undo her corset laces. Damnation!

Rosebud broke away long enough to catch a breath, but he pulled her back to him immediately, recklessly shoving down her loose bloomers and drawing her back into his amazing kiss. His hands cupped her bare bottom, urging her up into him.

She could feel the rigid length of him against her thigh, and she knew what they were moving toward. She didn't know whether she should be scared out of her wits or leaping into the fray. Leaping sounded a lot better at the moment. Yes, she was a tiny bit frightened, but she couldn't take much more of this heavy, sharp ache deep in her core that wouldn't go away. Hooking a leg around his hip, she arched into him, frantic with frustration and desire.

"Rose," he said gruffly, and she could feel the very

tip of him exactly where she needed him to be. He groaned. "You feel so damn good. This better not be a dream."

With her arms looped around his neck, she nibbled his lips, brushing kisses every which way, rubbing into him as best she could. "It's not a dream. I'm really here."

"But..." He stopped. He blinked. "It's not a dream?"

"Promise."

As if he were testing her, he reached out and touched her face. "Oh, my God." His eyes widened, and she could tell she was finally totally awake. He let go, scooting backward in the bed, almost pitching off the side. "You're real. Oh, my God. You're practically naked. Even more than before. You're not wearing any pants. And you're in my bed."

"You took off my pants," she told him, feeling bereft and cold without his hands or his mouth. "That much is your fault."

"I was asleep," he protested. "I thought I was dreaming."

"Well, you're not wearing any pants, either, and that was how you were when I got here, and you don't hear me complaining." As her gaze swept him up and down, her breath caught in her throat. "Oh, Ned. You are a sight to behold."

He yanked a pillow down over his lap. "I got into bed alone last night. I don't know how or when, but *you* climbed in with *me*. It's not my fault."

"Which part? The naked part? Or the, uh, hard part?" she asked in confusion, staring at his pillow. She smiled with mischief. "I think I'm willing to accept part of the blame for the hard part."

"Stop it, Rose. How did you get here? *When* did you get here?" He retreated from the bed entirely, still carefully holding the pillow over his midsection. Bending over awkwardly, he snatched his pants off the floor and tried to step into them without losing his pillow.

"Ned, don't be silly. I've already seen everything now."

She thought she was being so sensible and mature, pretending his nudity didn't faze her, but he didn't seem pleased. In fact, his expression only got darker.

"Who are you, Rose?" Ned zipped up his pants and tossed her her knickers. "Where have you been?"

"Since the other night, you mean?" Her heart did a small flip. "Does that mean you missed me?"

"No, it means since Tuesday night I've been wondering where the heck you disappeared to," he said impatiently. "You broke into my room then, too. And you vanished into thin air, remember?"

"Your fiancée was here. I could hardly stay," she said reasonably. "Since then... Well, I've been floating around, doing my job."

"Look, I know you're not really a maid. I saw the real maid yesterday. She'd never heard of you and she wasn't dressed like you, either."

"You asked about me?" She couldn't keep her lips from curving into a saucy smile. "Ned, you asked about me! With everything else you have going on, you were thinking about me. That's lovely."

"Rose, put on your clothes. Please? For my sanity."

She flushed a rosy shade of pink. She'd forgotten that her breasts and her bare limbs were hanging out down there. But she could hardly tell him that she wasn't used to having a body so she didn't notice when its clothes were missing. Well, except for the slight draft. Besides, she didn't want to put her clothes back on. She wanted Ned back in the bed, now, before she changed her mind.

One look at his stern face told her it was already too late. Quickly she tugged her camisole back into place, covering up her exposed breasts. Then she sat on the edge of the bed to button herself into her bloomers.

"Ned, I am sorry about last night," she offered. "I came to see you and you were already asleep. You looked so sweet that I..." Rosebud bit her lip. "All right, it's true. I climbed in with you and that was wrong of me. But it was just to be with you for a moment. It was the most beautiful thing I've ever felt."

His blue eyes took on a smoky hue.

She added, "I didn't plan to stay all night. I—I guess I fell asleep."

His gaze got even more heated. "So first you break and enter. Twice. And then you get in bed with me, start kissing me—" He broke off, swallowed and started again. "You kiss me, take off your clothes and come on to me. So we've moved from plain old burglar to stalker?"

"Oh, no," she corrected him. "I already told you— *you* kissed *me* and took off *my* clothes. Not vice versa." She wasn't exactly sure what "stalker" meant, but she had an idea. Not good. "I can't help it if you thought you were dreaming. You were very...persuasive."

"I'm a guy," he growled. "Any man who wakes up with a gorgeous, willing, half-naked woman in his bed is going to do exactly what I did."

"You think I'm gorgeous?" She was starting to feel melty and romantic again. Wondering if it would be possible to start again, she rose off the bed, but he backed away. Rosebud paused. "If any man would do exactly what you did, why did you stop?"

"Good question," he said darkly.

When he didn't elaborate, she frowned, crossing her arms over her camisole. She muttered, "I must be the world's worst excuse for a hooker."

Ned narrowed his eyes, but he advanced on her, taking her arm so that she couldn't move. "Is that what you are? A hooker? Soiled dove?"

"No!" she shot back. He was so infuriating! She felt like stamping her foot and throwing vases at his head. Too bad there were no vases handy. What could she say? *Well, I tried to become a soiled dove once, but it didn't work out. I died and became a ghost instead.*

But he was still suspicious. "You're sure nobody hired you to get into bed with me?"

"Of course I'm sure! If I were a real hooker," she added hotly, "I would know what to do to get you to make love to me instead of sending you running from my bed at the first opportunity."

"It was *my* bed."

"Sorry." Looking down at the place where his hand lay on her arm, Rosebud muttered, "It doesn't matter. I want you to know, I only came to check on you last night because of the altercation yesterday."

"What altercation? What are you talking about?"

"You," she said simply. "And Vanessa."

He stared at her. "You know about Vanessa?"

"Ned, she came to the door when I was here. Besides, this is a honeymoon hotel. I work here." She was proud of herself for actually telling the truth for once. She *did* work here. Just not the way he thought. "Of course I know that most of the men staying here are either married or engaged. I still haven't figured out why you and your fiancée are in separate rooms, however. That seems like a shameful waste of the Lady Godiva suite to me. Especially considering the twit could be sharing it with *you*."

But he was getting really steamed now. "Let me get this straight—you knew I was engaged and you still got into bed with me? You still wanted to fool around with me, knowing I'm supposed to marry somebody else in two days?" He glowered at her. "Rose, that's totally self-destructive. You shouldn't be sleeping with engaged men! What were you thinking?"

"I was thinking that she's a..." She trailed off.

"A what?" he prompted.

It was hard to think about anything except the fact that Ned was bare to the waist and standing so close, touching her. But he made her so angry.

"He's not looking at me too fondly at the moment, either, is he?" she grumbled, turning her face away from him.

Toting it up, in the two days she'd known him, he'd called her a burglar, a stripper, a hooker, a stalker, and maybe now just a garden variety floozy who thought it was fun to cheat with engaged men. Yes, well, if she got to pick, she'd choose to be a cheating floozy over being someone like Vanessa any day.

"What about Vanessa?" he repeated. "What were you going to say?"

"I will simply say that Vanessa is not a nice person," she offered grandly. "And you know what, Ned? She doesn't deserve you. After last night, that fact should be abundantly clear to you, too. She won't sleep with you or share her suite with you, she is bound and determined to push you into this marriage at the speed of light because she's afraid if you have time to think about it you will change your mind, she chats on her cell phone and ignores her guests, she complains about the servants right in front of them, not to mention she shouted at her sister and accused her of—"

He groaned loudly, cutting her off. "I don't know how you know all that, but I do not want to talk about Vanessa with you. That feels almost as wrong as waking up with you."

"It didn't feel wrong to me." Rosebud gazed at him, sure of how she felt in her heart. "It felt perfectly right."

The fire in his eyes grew hotter, less about anger, more about desire. When he moved his hand to brush back a tendril of her hair near her collarbone, she felt the usual sizzle of electricity. "Rose, I really need to know who you are and why you keep showing up in my room," he said in a husky growl. "You're driving me crazy with these games."

"That was never my intention," she managed to say. She closed her eyes and leaned into his hand. "Never."

"Everything about you is a mystery," he murmured, but he let his fingers tangle in her hair. "I don't know who you are or what you do at this hotel. I don't even know how you got out of my room the last time. But I can't seem to resist you."

"I just..." She sighed. "I just left. Like anybody else."

"No, that's not true," he whispered, winding the ringlet around his finger, forcing her even nearer. "When I came back, you were here. You kissed me."

"And it was wonderful, wasn't it?" She slid both

palms over his smooth, muscled chest. She couldn't get her fill of touching him.

But he set his own hands over hers, holding her still. Her face was so close to his that she could feel his breath puff hot against her cheek. "You were behind me when I answered the door. But when I turned around, you'd disappeared. Where did you go, Rose? How did you do that?"

"I hid in the closet."

"No, you didn't," he countered immediately. "The closet door was open. I could see there was no one in there."

"Then I must've hidden in the bathroom. It doesn't matter." She batted his hand away from her hair, starting to get antsy and dizzy standing so close. "Forget about me for a minute! Are you listening at all? The crucial thing here is your wedding. You need to call it off. It's tomorrow! There's no time. Call it off now."

"Rose, I—"

"No, listen. I forgot something important," she hastened to add. "Don't leave the hotel. Please don't leave the hotel. Call off the wedding. Yes, do that. But stay. In this room. I'm not asking for forever. Just a few days. Or a week. Two weeks. It could be like rest and recuperation for you after the stress of the breakup. Isn't that a good idea?"

He backed up slowly. "I don't understand why any of this is happening. It's like I fell into the Twilight Zone when I checked in here."

But Rosebud followed. She picked up steam, hoping she was actually getting through to him. "I understand that you're trying to be honorable and decent and good by not breaking things off with her, even if it is obvious to everyone that she's unsuitable. That's who you are, and I respect that, Ned. But you can't go through with something that is a mistake. Besides, is it really honorable or decent to spend the night with *me* when you're engaged to her?''

Ned's voice took on a harder edge when he noted, "You keep getting things backward, Rose. I didn't spend the night with you. You spent the night with me."

"Sometimes you're such a lawyer, Ned. It's infuriating!"

"I don't want to talk about Vanessa with you!" he said angrily. "I don't even want to think about Vanessa with you!"

"Then don't. Think about us instead. Ned, I saw how you looked at me," she whispered. "I felt how you touched me. It was in your eyes and in your fingers and especially in your kiss. You can't deny that there's a connection between us. I don't exactly understand it, either, but it's there."

His gaze held her. But he didn't deny it.

She raised her hand to his cheek. "You can't marry someone else when you feel this way about me."

"I can't feel this way about you when I don't know who you are," he muttered. Ned pushed away, crossing to his closet, where he pulled out a shirt. After a second, he took out another one and threw it over to her. "Put this on, will you? The way you dress... It's just part of this whole big equation. I can't handle it." He ran a hand through his hair, making the dark strands stick up in funny spikes. "I think I'm losing my mind."

Rosebud draped his shirt over her shoulders.

"You're not losing your mind. Just call off the wedding, Ned. You'll be amazed at how much better you feel."

Once again, he didn't answer.

There had to be a way to convince him. Meanwhile, she could feel her image starting to fade around the edges. *Uh-oh.* Visualization was hard to do and even harder to control. She was very good at it, far and away the best among Miss Arlotta's girls, but even she needed complete focus and concentration to make it last. With the emotional upheaval she'd been through this morning, it was no wonder she was having trouble.

All she needed was for one of her arms or legs to evaporate while Ned was watching. If he thought he was going crazy now, what would he do when she started disappearing in bits and pieces right before his eyes?

"I have to leave," she announced abruptly, heading for the door.

"Rose, don't go. You can't just waltz in here and make me nuts and then take off again."

"I have to go. Remember—call off the wedding. And don't leave the hotel."

But she had to get out of there. Feeling a little panicky, she raced past him, slipped out the door and slammed it behind her before he could follow. And then, with a great sense of relief, she immediately let herself sink into invisibility.

As she soared through the floorboards to return to her hiding place in the attic, Rosebud realized she was still wearing Ned's shirt. Inhaling the scent of him, wrapping it closer around her, she crawled onto the chaise in her alcove, desperate for a nap.

Being visible—and being in love—really took it all out of a girl.

Thursday night

SOMEHOW—HE WASN'T EXACTLY sure how—Ned had stumbled from one thing to the next, ending up at his bachelor party exactly on time. Considering his mental state, that was practically a miracle.

The funny thing was that none of his friends, not even his best man, Chris, seemed to have noticed he was in such a strange, moody frame of mind. Not at all appropriate for a stag party.

Ned frowned.

After Rose had left, he'd been furious with her and with himself that she had the power to get under his skin so completely. This just didn't happen to men like him, who planned their lives ahead, who thought long and hard and always picked the wisest choice, who knew where they should be at any given moment. And with whom.

Good God! He'd almost made love to her. To some lunatic who traipsed around barefoot, breaking into hotel rooms, getting in bed with the guests, all the while dressed in strange, skimpy lingerie that looked like it was rescued off the Titanic! Was she an escapee from a mental hospital? An escapee with a fetish for old-fashioned underwear?

And why couldn't he stop thinking about her?

"Maybe because she pops in and out like the Ghost of Christmas Past."

Or maybe because her skin was the softest thing he'd ever touched, she smelled like roses, she looked at him with those shining eyes that told him he could do no wrong, and every time he was near her, she sparked a fire that would not quit. He wanted her so badly his bones ached.

Weirder yet, there was something genuine about her he really liked. It was a dangerous combination, that kind of potent desire and sweet affection. Even if she was the oddest woman he'd ever met.

"Damn it." Setting his cigar aside, he tossed back two fingers of Scotch, enjoying the burn as it streaked down his throat. Here he was, at his own bachelor party, with his best friends around him, the night before his wedding to Vanessa. And all he had on his mind was Rose.

About a minute and a half after she'd left this morning, he'd decided he had to go after her. But when he opened the door and stomped out in the hallway, she wasn't there. Not a sign of her.

Once again, she'd managed to vanish without a trace. Well, there was one trace. She'd left her glasses behind on the windowsill. Ned patted his jacket pocket. Still there. She had to be real and not a figment of his fevered imagination if she'd left her glasses behind. And now she'd have to come back for them, wouldn't she?

"I'm not the crazy one. She is," he growled, pulling the cigar back to his mouth, giving it a good chomp. "Or maybe she's just a magician. Who else pulls disappearing acts like that?"

"Ned? You planning to smoke that thing or just kill it?" Chris inquired dryly. "This is a party, not your execution. You might at least make some feeble attempt to enjoy yourself."

"Sorry."

"Okay. Apology accepted. Now could you maybe get out of your chair, put on a smile and socialize?" His best man leaned in closer. "Everyone is starting to wonder about you."

"Yeah, well, I'm starting to wonder about myself," he allowed as he lit the stogie and took a puff or two.

"Wedding bell blues, huh?"

"You could say that."

Chris paused for a second. "Don't take this the wrong way, but... Is there another woman?"

He must've inhaled too quickly, because he started to choke on the smoke from his cigar.

"I'll take that as a yes," his friend joked, pounding him on the back.

"It's not what you think."

"Never is, buddy. Never is."

"No, but... I'm not some dog who sleeps around while he's engaged," he said stubbornly. "I take commitments very seriously."

"I know that. I know you pretty well after all these years." Chris pulled up a chair. "Does Vanessa know there's someone else?"

"No. God, no." That was all he needed, for Vanessa to find out.

Any hope of a nice, sane, reasonable delay for the wedding—a compromise they could both live with, enough to give him some time to breathe—would be out the window if Vanessa had any hint he was cheating. Not that there was any hope of that, anyway. He knew compromise was a pipe dream when it came to this hasty rush toward a wedding.

"So who is she?"

"I don't know who she is or where she came from," he said slowly. "I just met her Tuesday, here at the hotel. She keeps showing up when I least expect her and then disappearing again."

"Uh-huh." Chris edged his chair closer, puffing on his own cigar.

"I think she may not be all there," he admitted, thinking out loud more than anything else. "You know, mentally? There's something really odd about her."

Chris's voice took on a sarcastic edge. "Okay, so this sounds promising. You met a crazy chick, you don't know who she is or where she came from, you think you may be in love with her, and—"

"I didn't say that," he protested. "I've only seen her twice. And I haven't slept with her." Well, actually, he *had* slept with her. He just hadn't had sex with her. He didn't plan to share that information with his best man, however. "A few kisses. That's it."

Chris arched an eyebrow. "You met her Tuesday and you've already made out with her, all the while you were both staying in the same hotel with your fiancée? You've always been good, but man, that's *good*, even for you. Hot and cold running women in a honeymoon hotel. How did you manage that?"

"Okay, stop it right now. I didn't manage anything. It just happened. It didn't mean anything." Brooding over his own deceit, Ned took a long draw on the cigar. "My problems with Vanessa are separate from Rose."

"So she has a name. And you're sure this cold feet

thing doesn't have anything to do with her?" his friend asked shrewdly. "I mean, maybe your girl Rose is a symptom. Ned, anybody who knows you knows it is so not like you to go picking up some crazy chick two days before your wedding. Yeah, you had your wild days, but you were always unattached. Whenever you were with one woman, you stayed with one woman."

"I know, but..." Ned took another gulp of Scotch. "Don't call her a crazy chick."

"Oh, man. This is bad. So what are you going to do? You can't call off the wedding. My God, Vanessa will give you a blowup that'll make Vesuvius look like a bottle rocket." Chris signaled the waiter to bring him another drink. "And you have never been one for blowups."

"I know."

"So let me ask you this. Do you love Vanessa? Do you want to be married to her?"

"I don't know."

"Okay, that answers that," his best man said sagely. "No and no." He shook his head. "Well, my man, completely aside from the crazy chick...aside from this new woman, I think you've got to get out of it. I have to admit, since you were the last one of the guys to hold out, I was looking forward to you being married, too. Last man standing, you know? But if it isn't right—and brother, you look miserable—then it isn't right."

"Bring on Vesuvius, huh? Yeah, that's a plan." He leaned back in his chair with a sigh, blowing smoke rings high above his head.

"The real question is how and when," Chris decided. "Do you want to do a J.Lo and Ben and call it off at the last minute? Or a Britney, go ahead and get married, and then quietly end it five minutes later?"

Ned groaned, dropping his head into his hands. "I don't want either of those choices. Believe me, I have no desire to act like J.Lo, Ben or Britney. How did I get myself into this mess?"

"I don't know. I've been wondering that myself." Chris patted him on the shoulder. "Listen, if it were me, I would have a few drinks, mingle, put it out of my mind tonight. Have a good time, you know? You've got until the minister asks you to say 'I Do' to make up your mind. Considering who you're dumping, I don't think the timing is going to make it that much worse."

"Thanks for the advice, Chris."

"No charge. It's part of the best man package."

Ned smiled for the first time that night. "Thanks, anyway."

"Oh, and Ned? Don't leave before the stripper gets here. She's supposed to be something special." Sticking his cigar back in his mouth, his friend checked his watch. "Hey, my stripper is late. Wonder what's up with that?"

Ned didn't care. He'd never been that interested in strippers, anyway. How special could this one be?

7

STRETCHING LANGUIDLY, Rose yawned. Oh, she was wearing Ned's shirt. Wasn't that sweet? She turned up the collar, enjoying the eau de real man scent one more time.

Hmm... It seemed awfully dark in her garret, even for a place without windows. What time had it gotten to be, anyway? She peered down at her VCR.

"My stars!" she exclaimed, sitting up on her settee and taking a gander at the little green numbers on the VCR display. "It's after eight! How long was I asleep?"

This was very strange. Yes, materializing was a strain and most of the girls who tried it needed naps afterward, but...twelve hours?

"Good heavens, I was only visible for an hour or so! How can this be?"

Well, it was too late to worry about it. She had work to do, relationships to break up, grooms to seduce. And a formidable boss to get around.

Since nobody had been calling her name or waking her up out of her sound sleep to drag her in front of the council, she figured she was still basking in the glow of her new gold star. Thank goodness, the Inn was so busy. Everybody's couples must be causing major problems, because Miss A didn't usually do shoddy work.

"She's going to find out sooner or later that Ned and Vanessa weren't anywhere near passion last night." Rosebud's lips curved into a self-satisfied smile. "Whereas Ned and I actually got fairly close to it this morning."

A while ago, she'd watched this silly movie where this nun went spinning around in a meadow, singing her little heart out. For the first time, Rosebud actually understood how she felt. After getting to spend the night with Ned, even if it didn't end as well as it could've, Rosebud truly felt like throwing out her arms and spinning in a meadow. Maybe even singing.

Okay, time to get cracking. First up, a makeover. She refused to go another minute in that ridiculous outfit. That was what she was wearing when she passed over, and they'd all assumed they were stuck in those outfits for eternity, but Rosebud knew better. After all, Miss Arlotta changed her outfits all the time. Of course, Miss Arlotta had lots of powers nobody else enjoyed, but still...Rosebud figured she ought to be able to handle the clothing thing. She'd experimented with changing the ribbons in her hair with some success, and now knew she could take off her bloomers, at least when she was completely three-dimensional.

She needed to practice this clothes-changing thing if she was going to pop up and see Ned. So she materialized again, took off Ned's shirt, then peeled off the rest of her clothes, too.

"Naked is fairly easy. But how do I make new clothes?"

She wished she had a mirror so she could try on some different things. Peering at her reflection in the front of her television set, she realized suddenly that she wasn't wearing her glasses.

"Oh, no. I left them on Ned's windowsill." She calmed herself. "It's okay. As soon as I put some clothes on, that will be my first stop. I can check on Ned and get my spectacles back. Until then, the world will have a hazy, romantic glow. That's not such a bad thing."

Back to clothes. First, underwear. She made a mental picture of some pretty panties and a bra she'd seen in a magazine. Nothing happened. She found the magazine, stared at the pictures till her eyes watered and tried again. Still nothing.

"Oh, fiddlesticks!" Squeezing her eyes shut, she focused all her concentration on that silly bra and panties, willing them to appear on her body. Pop. She opened her eyes. And there they were. "Ha! I'm *good!* They can keep their silly gold stars. I can materialize like nobody's business and I can even make clothes!"

She set about creating an outfit for herself, wishing she'd thought of this fashion thing years ago. She took a pale-pink outfit out of a magazine—something some teen princess had worn to pick up an award—and a pair of pink sandals off a different page.

"All right then," she said, pulling the red ribbons out of her ringlets and finger-combing her hair, trying to do something more modern with it. "First I'll go check on Ned and make sure he's okay. Not show up, just check. No touching. No kissing. All aboveboard. Maybe he's even discarded the odious Vanessa by now. Wouldn't that be lovely?" She allowed herself to savor that thought for a moment. "Next I will look in

on her, nip in the bud any trouble she might be thinking of causing... And maybe then I can go back to Ned
and show off my new outfit. Maybe he'd like to help
me out of it.''

Her smile widened. Ah, the joys of being a smart,
high-spirited ghost who took matters into her own
hands.

But when she swept down to Ned's room, her tri-
umph began to fade. He wasn't there. And neither
were her glasses.

At least he hadn't checked out. She knew those were
still his clothes in the closet, his toiletries on the vanity
in the bathroom.

''Maybe he's breaking up with Vanessa right this
minute,'' she told herself. And she flashed over to the
Lady Godiva Suite, hoping for the best.

Vanessa was there, all right, but still no Ned. Rosebud hung back, taking stock. What was this all about?

Romantic music, heavy on the strings, emanated
from the CD player. The lamps had been dimmed,
with a pair of candles the only light in the parlor of the
suite. There were flowers, chocolates, cheese and fruit,
and champagne on ice. Vanessa had already popped
the cork and she was strolling around, humming to
herself, sipping bubbly from a crystal flute. Another
glass was set out near the silver bucket.

She was in an awfully jolly mood, wasn't she? Rosebud didn't like the looks of that.

She had to admit, Vanessa had made an effort. And
it had worked pretty well, for her. The Wicked Witch
was wearing a slinky white dress, and Rosebud could
tell she didn't have anything on underneath it. No

shoes, either. Instead of pulling back her hair into the usual smooth chignon, she'd left it loose, maybe even crimped it.

What was going on here?

Vanessa picked up the phone. "Room service?" she said after a moment. "I'll need more champagne. Cristal 1973. At least one more bottle and two if you can find them. And make it snappy."

After hanging up, she frowned, straightening one of the white roses in her floral arrangement. Then she busied herself writing a note on a piece of hotel stationery she'd pulled from a drawer in the desk.

Rosebud tried to hover close enough behind her to read what she'd written, but all she saw was something that looked like *Come right up.* Vanessa folded the note paper, stuck it in an envelope and scrawled *Ned* in big letters on the front.

Not much mystery there. It seemed Ned's fiancée was sending him a royal summons to run up to her suite for a little seduction scene. Her sultry clothes, her hair, the music and champagne… Not exactly subtle.

As Rosebud brooded, there was a knock on the door. "Room service," someone called out.

Vanessa let him in, ordered him to put the extra champagne in the refrigerator, and then she gave him the note she'd written. "I need you to take this note down to my fiancé," she ordered in a no-nonsense tone. She seemed kind of jumpy and ill at ease. "You can do that, can't you? He's at his bachelor party in the billiard room, wherever that is."

"I know where it is, ma'am."

"Good." She handed him a fifty-dollar bill. "I think

they're expected to go quite late, but I'd like you to take this note to him now. Ned Mulgrew. He's tall, dark hair, very handsome. Shouldn't be hard to spot since he is, after all, the groom. I think they've ordered a stripper or something, so he'll be the one with a stripper in his lap and tassels in his face."

Vanessa sneered when she said "stripper." She didn't seem to appreciate the value of a stripper at a stag party, and for once, Rosebud actually agreed with her. Who would send a dancer who took her clothes off to entertain *Ned?* And what was that bit about tassels?

Meanwhile, why was he at this bachelor party to start out with? Why hadn't he called off this farce of an engagement yet?

Her mood quickly went from bad to worse. Vanessa plotting a seduction, Ned with tassels in his face, and everybody still going full speed ahead toward this idiotic wedding!

"I don't think so," Rosebud said with spirit. "Not while I'm around."

She whipped out of that suite so fast it created a backdraft, blowing out Vanessa's candles. As the Wicked Witch swore under her breath and relit them, Rosebud headed for the billiard room.

But she skidded to a stop inside the door. The dark, smoky billiard room, tucked into a corner on the long hall of the west wing, was full of men and free-flowing liquor, an elaborate carved mahogany bar that had been there forever, loud music, several games of darts and pool, but no stripper with or without tassels. Good.

Squinting, she located Ned fairly quickly. He was

sitting in a chair, looking morose. He had a drink in one hand and a cigar in the other, and he appeared to be getting a real talking-to from his father, who was standing next to him, pointing at him with one finger. Rosebud wafted closer.

"You need to get yourself together," Jack Mulgrew commanded, jabbing that finger in the air. "You aren't backing out. Too late. Nobody does that to a woman. It's ugly."

"Wouldn't it be uglier to marry someone I don't love and then divorce her in six months or a year?" Ned asked quietly.

Good point, Ned!

"That isn't how things are done," his father spit out. "You know that. Part of this is business, Ned. It's bad business to string along a Westicott and then humiliate her."

His words were a tad slurred when he said, "I don't care about the business. This is my life."

"It isn't going to be much of a life if you're a social pariah, Westicott pulls all his business out of your law firm, Mulgrew Media loses the merger, and no woman in Denver is willing to go near you." Mr. Mulgrew shook his head from side to side. "You're a smart guy, Ned. Don't be incredibly stupid now. Suck it up, do what needs to be done, make your family proud."

Ned sloshed down whiskey from the tumbler in his hand.

"It would be different if you had someone else," his father lectured. "But you don't. And let's face it, nothing has changed since July when you decided to propose to her. You said to me then that you were thirty, you'd dated a lot of nice women, and it wasn't like the perfect one was suddenly going to show up. Your words, Ned."

"I remember."

"You have to move on and be an adult at some point. Marry Vanessa. Have some kids. Take your life to the next level. It's time, Ned."

"Uh, Ned?" Thank goodness the best man chose that moment to interrupt the unpleasant father-son conversation. Chris handed over the note Rosebud recognized was from Vanessa. "Somebody from room service came by and asked me to give this to you. I think it's from Vanessa. Oh, and I checked on the stripper. She got lost or something, but she's here now, so if you can hang on, the main event will start shortly." He glanced between Ned and his dad. "Everything okay?"

"Yeah, we're fine. Get my father another drink, will you?" Ned rose from his chair. "I'm going to read my mail here, see what Van wants, and then circulate, maybe play some pool." He smiled as he pushed past his friend. "And yes, Chris, I will be front and center for your stripper. I won't leave till after she performs. I promise."

"Ned," his dad called behind him. "Think about what I said."

"Don't need to. I've already got it." He slipped into the crowd, opening the note from Vanessa.

Oh, dear. This was getting dire. Ned, pressured by his father to do the right thing (which she thought was exactly the wrong thing) and then pressured by Vanessa to come up and play bedroom games.

"I wonder how drunk he is. I wonder how much he cares what his father thinks," Rosebud pondered.

Vanessa was lying in wait upstairs. The stripper was in the wings, and her performance was the only thing keeping Ned down here, away from the spider. First things first. Delay the stripper.

"Better yet, put her out of the picture entirely," Rosebud murmured with satisfaction. No need to add some other chippie to this already complicated mix.

She swooped through the main floor, scanning the lobby and the restaurant and three different restrooms before she located a rather confused-looking woman outside bathroom #4. The woman was wearing a raincoat with tall white stiletto heels and a tiny bridal veil tucked into her hair. She was also carrying a boom box. Rosebud ducked around the corner and closed her eyes, focusing long enough to get her body together, before stepping out from behind her pillar.

"Excuse me," she said politely, tapping the woman on the shoulder. "You wouldn't be the stripper for the Mulgrew party, would you? I'm with the hotel. They sent me to find you and take you to the billiard room."

"Oh. Okay. Yeah, I'm the one. I'm more of a dancer than a stripper, actually." She flashed open her raincoat, revealing a pair of silver tassels, exactly as Vanessa had predicted, one stuck onto the center of each large breast, and what appeared to be a short, stiff white petticoat with garters and stockings. That was it. "See, I don't take anything else off. I just pop out of the cake and dance like this. So, technically, I'm not a stripper. I just dance."

Rosebud's eyes grew wide. How in the world did

that girl and those breasts fit inside a cake? Who baked
it? And how? Did people eat it after a woman had been
inside it?

"You don't know where it is, do you?" the dancer
asked. "It should be around here somewhere. Once I'm
inside the cake, somebody has to wheel me into the
party and start my boom box. You know, for my music." She lifted it to demonstrate.

"Wait, you're looking for a cake? Wouldn't it be in
the restaurant kitchen?" Rosebud asked helpfully.

"No. I mean, it's not a real cake. It's plywood. With
layers. Like a wedding cake. It's yellow, because my
name, you know, is Lemon Chiffon."

Once again, Rosebud was speechless. And she'd
thought Desdemoaner was a terrible name. "Really?"

Miss Chiffon looked very dubious. "No. I made it
up. Lemon Chiffon? Like the cake?"

"Oh, I see."

"It's got a lid. You know, so I can pop out."

"Okay, well, I was told to take you downstairs," she
said, tugging the woman along by her boom box. "This
way. Maybe your cake is down here."

It was remarkably easy to lead her down to the base-
ment, right into the wine cellar, grab the boom box,
give her a shove and lock her in there. Switching back
to invisibility, Rosebud told herself, "Somebody will
come by sooner or later. Miss Chiffon will be fine.
Maybe there's even a corkscrew in there."

No time to worry about the cake dancer. Rosebud
knew she had to hurry. She popped back up to Vanessa's suite, used her magic with electronics to get a
blaze going in the fireplace, turned up the thermostat

and conjured up "Lullabies for Fussy Babies" and "Songs to Sleep By" to stick in the CD player.

She noticed the first champagne bottle was empty, and moved the second into the ice bucket. A whole bottle of champagne, all by herself? Vanessa ought to be good and sloshed.

"Just keep drinking, princess."

Not that she had any intention of letting the prince get back here, anyway. But if he did, all he would find was a locked door, a hot, stuffy suite, a snoring, passed-out princess, and a couple of empty champagne bottles. If he ever got back there. If she had her way, he would find himself headed a different direction entirely.

Rosebud bolted the door, unplugged the phone and flew back downstairs as quickly as she could get there.

Outside the wine cellar, she collected the boom box, took a moment to compose herself, pressed her eyes closed and tried to concentrate on conjuring up an outfit she found appropriate for a girl who jumped out of cakes. Something better than a tiny bridal veil, two tassels and a few inches of organza, please. She was almost surprised when she opened her eyes and looked down at herself.

She saw a red velvet corset with excellent cleavage, and down below, black stockings and adorable little black, high-heeled boots. She even had black ruffled panties under her tiny black skirt. She wasn't sure if she looked more like someone from that *Moulin Rouge* movie or the scandalous woman who'd played the Palace in Denver when she was twelve.

Whomever, it was showtime. "Nobody can say I don't give it my all," she said bravely.

Now all she had to do was find that cake.

NED TRIED to manufacture a smile when he saw a couple of waiters carry in the enormous painted cake on a wheeled cart. Oh, well. It was cheesy, but at least it was kind of funny. As they cleared a space for the cart, pulling their chairs around, somebody set a boom box on the bar and hit Play, signaling the entertainment was due to begin.

The guys were loud and boisterous, and it was hard to hear the music. Ned sat back in his chair, trying to be a good sport. Man, he hated being the center of attention when it came to things like this. People were whooping it up and slapping him on the back, teasing him about what was coming, and he did his part, grinning like an idiot.

At first, the music from the boom box sounded vaguely like "I'm Too Sexy," but after a bar or two, it took a very different turn. He'd never heard anything like that. Wheezy, high-pitched and full of static, it sounded as if it were cranking out of an old player piano.

And then the top of the cake slapped open, a small hand in a long black glove came out with it, and out popped...

"Rose?" he choked.

Everybody in the room was cheering lustily as she stood there, still partially in the cake, her arms flung into the air. She winked at Ned, and he felt paralyzed, pinned to his seat with shock and horror. Could anybody tell he knew her? Did Chris suspect she was the one?

He slugged down the last of his Scotch and the ice cube came with it, almost lodging in his throat. He didn't care. Let him die right there, strangled by an ice cube. Lord, this was bizarre. First he wasn't sure she really existed because he was the only one who saw her. And now she was in front of thirty guys, jumping out of a freaking cake!

Just like the other two times he'd seen her, she was wearing a corset, but this one was red. And there was no other top under it, so her creamy, round curves were all there, mounded up against the deep-red velvet. He felt the familiar, undeniable pull toward her, even as he fought to control himself and his urges. His hands twisted into fists. If he hadn't held himself back, he'd already have stalked over, yanked her off that rickety wooden cake, carried her upstairs and made love to her for about a week. Maybe two.

Her eyes were sparkling, her smile was wicked and she started singing something about "Ze Naughty Folies Bergeres." She kicked out one black stocking, going for a kind of can-can thing, whipping up her frisky little skirt, singing, "At ze Folies Bergere, my feet, zey fly up in ze air!"

Whirling around, she showed off her bottom in a pair of ruffly black panties. Ned groaned. The panties got a definite reaction from the crowd, which made him feel like cheerfully punching the lights out of every single man in the room. She blew him a kiss. He clenched his jaw.

"Pretty good, huh?" Chris asked, bashing him on the shoulder.

"Yeah, great," he managed.

"Oooh la la!" she called out, clambering out of the cake with help from three or four guys. They set her down on the floor a few feet in front of Ned, where she pulled off one of her long black gloves, one centimeter at a time, and draped it around his neck. She ripped the other one off fast, tossing it into the crowd.

Then she backed away, singing in a throaty, sexy whisper about all the trouble you could get into in France if you had a mind to. She was rolling her r's into some kind of purr that slid right up his spine. As for her dance, well, it wasn't the most accomplished thing he'd ever seen, but she was obviously enjoying herself.

There were hoots and whistles and calls for her to take off more clothes as she continued to play the sassy siren, while Ned didn't know how to react. Yes, it was sexy. Yes, he still wanted her. But part of him wanted to turn her over his knee and spank her, too, for driving him crazy like this. Besides, tonight he wasn't the only one attracted to Rose. Every man there wanted to get his hands on her.

She danced closer, and now she was doing the sexy purr directly to him. One small hand grazed his cheek, she twirled to the other side, catching his knee, and then she was in front of him again, bending over, displaying a whole lot of beautiful skin. The view was for his eyes only. Whether that made it better or worse, he had no idea. He wasn't functioning very well at the moment. With no help from him—he was still hanging on with all his might to the ragged edges of his self-control—she climbed into his lap and pulled on both ends of the glove that was still hanging around his neck, dragging his face up close to hers.

"Aw, Ned," she whispered, "you don't look happy to see me."

"What do you think you're doing, Rose?" he asked darkly.

"Trying to get a rise out of you," she told him sweetly, kicking up her legs and wiggling in his lap. "Oooh la la!"

"If you don't sit still, you're going to get more than a rise out of me," he gritted between his teeth.

"Good." When she shifted in his lap, dipping her head, bringing her lips half an inch from his, the light in her eyes changed from mischief to something more dangerous. "I figured if I popped out of your cake, you couldn't ignore me."

"When have I ever ignored you?"

She didn't answer, but dropped the glove, set her hands on his cheeks and lowered her mouth to his.

Her kiss was chaste and innocent, just a light press of her lips to his, but Ned had reached his limit. His hands shoved up into her hair before he could stop himself. He held her head fast, forcing her to go deeper, exploring her mouth and her tongue, devouring her sweetness and her heat. He actually saw stars. Or maybe that was because he was more intent on ravishing her mouth than remembering to breathe.

The kiss seemed to go on forever, but he had no intention of breaking away. She was the best thing he'd ever tasted. Somewhere in his periphery, he heard murmurs and laughter, even jeers.

"Ned." His father knocked him on the shoulder. "That's enough."

"Aw, come on," somebody else yelled. "It's his bachelor party. His last chance. The groom is supposed to make it with the stripper. It's tradition."

Rose pulled back then. Her lips looked rosy and swollen, and she was breathing hard. "Ned?"

He didn't know what answer she wanted. Did she expect him to tell people that she was more than just the stripper, that she wasn't some quick grope at a stag party? This was her game, not his. She was the one who'd jumped out of the cake and into his lap.

The overhead lights in the smoky billiard parlor flickered suddenly, off and on, then off again, plunging the place into darkness. "Last call?" somebody asked, but the bartender answered, "Nah, I didn't do it. Must be a power surge or something. Hang tight. I'm sure we'll get the lights back on."

"Hey, Ned," his dad called out. "Don't go anywhere. I need to talk to you."

Rose shoved away from Ned, scrambling off his lap. There were too many people and it was too dark in there. He couldn't see where she was headed, but he knew it had to be for the door. Where else was she going to go? He was not going to let her vanish one more time.

The lights were still on in the corridor outside the billiard room, and he caught a flash of her red costume as she cleared the door. Ned rushed to follow. He caught her hand.

"I think I made a mistake, Ned," she whispered. Her eyes were huge and hazy green. "This turned into something different. I was trying to have some fun. And maybe distract you. From her. I didn't intend to..."

"Bring it all out in the open? Ruin my life?"

She swallowed. "Make myself look like a whore."

"Aw, Rose." That hit him where he lived. "You could never look like that." He tipped a finger under her chin, forcing her to meet his gaze. "Not a chance."

"There are so many things you don't know," she whispered.

"So tell me. Fill me in," he shot back. "It's not like I haven't asked."

Rose reached up to kiss him again, quick and sweet. "We can talk later, Ned. Right now, we need to get out of here before your father figures out you left with me. What do you want to do? Where do you want to go? What about Vanessa?"

"That's the million-dollar question." He'd forgotten Vanessa's message until Rose mentioned her. How odd. The note was stuck in his jacket pocket next to Rose's glasses.

But he already knew the answer. With Rose...there was no such thing as free will. He was under a spell, bewitched, bedazzled. Nothing else existed. He pulled the paper out of his pocket and crumpled it into a ball. And then he threw it aside.

"So you're coming with me?"

"Yes," he decided. "Yes. Let's get out of here."

The lights from the billiard parlor flooded back on behind them, but Rose took his hand and tugged him the other direction. "This way," she said quickly. "No one will see us. Follow me."

It was the strangest thing. Down the hall, skirting around the lobby, into a small parlor in the back, Rose led him along without saying a word. The parlor was dark, but he could see it was decorated in a lot of red velvet, with antiques and books everywhere. Rose walked straight to a bookshelf, jerked on a specific volume and waited till a panel opened up right beside her.

"A secret passage?" he asked in disbelief. "You're kidding."

"It's been here a long time," she told him as she stepped into the narrow opening, motioning for him to follow. Just inside the passageway, she turned back. "Ned, this is your last chance for a detour. From here, you can go straight outside to the alley. That's how important customers used to escape if the police made a visit to the bordello or the speakeasy it turned into."

"Why would I want to go to the alley?"

"Because your only other choice is to come upstairs. With me." She licked her lip. "Once we're in the passage, there's no turning back. Which will it be?"

Ned caught her around the waist and bent down to kiss her, hard. "When it comes to you, I can't help myself. I can't turn back. Upstairs. Let's go."

8

NED WAS IN A HURRY, that much seemed clear. In a hurry to get upstairs to her room and into her bed.

They hadn't spelled out where exactly she was taking him or what would happen once they got there, but they both knew.

Starting to feel dizzy with anticipation, Rosebud raced up the narrow, curving stairs ahead of him, trying to go faster. It had been so long since she'd been with a man, all the way, and from what she could tell from movies and books, people were a bit freer and more adventurous now. Would she be able to keep up?

Ned was right behind her at every turn, squeezing her hand, pushing her along. Maybe it was because his body was so close and the space so confined, maybe it was the heady prospect of what lay ahead, or maybe because she wasn't accustomed to actually *walking* up stairs anymore, especially tiny, uneven stairs that wound around like this, but she lost her footing several times. Trembling, flushed with annoyance, she cursed her own clumsiness under her breath.

They were never going to get up to the attic if she kept tripping. And if they didn't get there soon, she thought she might explode from pent-up desire.

As she tried to focus on putting one foot in front of the other, quickly, Rosebud couldn't forget how close he was, looming over her, brushing her, making fleeting contact. His hand grasped hers, his fingers grazed her hip or her hair, his eyes lingered on the pale curve of her breast...

But it wasn't enough. More of Ned, less of Ned... Something had to change, fast.

The staircase got skinnier, darker and even more curvy as she navigated their way nearer the top, but she kept scrambling forward, trying to pick up the pace. A few more steps. A few more turns.

"Oof," she mumbled, taking a treacherous bend too quickly, completely pitching forward onto the next step. Once again, Ned was there, solid and secure, blocking her from falling back down the stairs. But this time he lifted her close up against him for a long moment, balancing himself against the sloping wall, crumpling her skirt under his arm as he gripped her tight around the waist. It was dark and silent in the passage, and she could hear her own heartbeat, taste the whiskey on his hot, ragged breath, feel the unyielding barrier of his body behind and around her.

"How big a secret is this staircase?" he whispered, rubbing his cheek against her hair. "How many people know about it?"

"A few. Why?" she asked, closing her eyes, shivering at the delicious feel of the front of his long thigh folding into the back of hers.

"I wondered what the odds were anyone would know if we..."

"If we...?"

With one arm still hard around her waist, he slid his hand up to cup her bottom, finding her ruffled panties, hooking his thumb under the edge. It was a good thing he was holding her up, because she couldn't have stood on her own, not with his fingers teasing her, plucking at her ruffles, slipping around to test the lace at the top of her black thigh-high stocking, dancing away.

His voice was rough and urgent when he said, "It's dark in here. It's private. And I've had the most unbelievable view of your cute little butt coming up a whole lot of stairs. A man can only take so much."

Impatient, he tugged down her panties, exposing the round curve of one cheek. His roving hand, her bare flesh...

Desire flooded to her core. Rosebud's mouth dropped open as air suddenly seemed impossible to come by. She gasped, "Here?"

"Yes, here."

Her whole body felt moist and warm, incredibly, painfully aroused, and her legs had turned to water. She couldn't climb one more step, even if she'd wanted to. "Yes," she breathed, twisting in his arms, sinking back onto the steps. Half sitting, half lying, she reached for him. "I want you, Ned. I want you now."

It was all the invitation he needed. Levering himself on top of her, he kissed her quick and fierce, nipping at her lips. They were both shoving at each other's clothes, too eager to be careful. She grabbed his shirt-front, popping buttons in her haste, pushing away his jacket and shirt, sighing with bliss as she slid her palms across his firm, muscled abdomen and chest, trying to get to his belt buckle. At the same time, he tore down her skirt and panties, carelessly stripping them off over her stockings and boots. Then he concentrated on the red velvet bustier, taking his time with each hook down her front.

Frustrated at her attempts with his buckle, Rosebud swore at the stupid thing. Her hands shook, making it impossible to get him out of his pants. She lay back, quivering with agitation as he freed her from her stiff, tight bodice, one maddening hook at a time.

"Stay still," he ordered. "This isn't easy."

"Hurry," she told him. "Hurry."

The raw truth was that she needed him. She needed him now. For all she knew her body would fade before his eyes, Miss Arlotta would snatch her away for her wickedness, or the whole Inn would spontaneously burst into flames. She was so terribly afraid that she would never, ever get a chance to satisfy this aching, pulsing hunger.

Dripping wet, shameless, desperate, she arched up into him, willing him to take her. *Now.* He had most of it undone. Her breasts were free. It was just her waist. Who cared if she couldn't breathe?

"Leave the corset," she pleaded. "Please? Hurry!"

"No." Batting her hands away, he yanked the last of the hooks free, opening up the heavy corset like a Christmas package. He grinned at her as he eased it away, sliding one hand up her smooth stomach, tweaking her breast, staring down at her with undisguised lust. He bent and licked her from one nipple all the way down to her navel and all she could do was whimper.

Then he wrenched his belt through the buckle, hastily tore down his zipper and kicked away his trousers and briefs. Somehow he'd already lost his shoes and socks. She didn't even see that happen. Her own stockings and boots were still in place, however, and it appeared they were going to stay there. Rosebud gulped. The look in Ned's eyes told her everything she needed to know. *I can't turn back.*

She swallowed around a parched throat as her gaze swept up and down his lean body, drinking in the elegant angles and rigid planes. The light was dim, he was partially obscured by the crazy position they were in on the staircase, but she knew what she saw. Ned was magnificent.

He fitted his body next to hers, tracing the line of her shoulder and her hip and her breast with his whole hand, and she closed her eyes, melting into him. As his mouth covered hers, Ned's fingers eased between her thighs, rubbing her tiny, shivering nub.

Stunned, she understood for the first time how much better this was in person than in a movie. Her eyes flew open. This was the first time she'd... "Ohhh!" she cried, unable to stop her body from clenching and rising into his rhythm.

Everything started to sizzle and spin. Her vision was getting fuzzy around the edges. Was she still here? Oh, God, don't let her disappear now, in the middle of this, with desire tied up like a hard knot inside her, with his fingers stroking, pushing...

Suddenly everything broke loose at once, and if he hadn't been on top of her, she would've tumbled down the stairs with the shocking, rocketing sensation.

"Wow," she murmured. "Wow." She ran a hand through his soft, dark hair, overwhelmed with tenderness and passion mixed together. It was the most out-rageous thing to have all these emotions spilling to-gether. She was giddy from it. She should've been embarrassed to be so noisy in her appreciation, so ea-ger and unschooled, so greedy for more while the shudders still echoed inside her. But she wasn't. She was just happy.

As she linked her arms around his neck, rubbing her breasts into his chest and her belly against the rigid, velvety length of his manhood, she laughed with the sheer joy she felt. Ned set her stocking-clad legs around his hips, slowly, ruthlessly nudging himself closer to her moist core. Why didn't he plunge inside? She wanted him so badly. She wiggled enough to try to ease him in, but still he held back, giving her an inch, no more. Her laughter died as a gasp of mixed frustra-tion and pleasure escaped her instead.

Pleasure? Again? Could you do that twice? Oh, yes, you could. The shivers and quakes were already climb-ing, and he hadn't even gotten started.

"Please," she moaned, wiggling, writhing, desperate to pull him deeper. "Ned, I didn't know... *Please*."

And then he finally relented, sliding deep inside, with a long, powerful stroke that sent her reeling. Hot, hard, insistent, he pounded into her again and again as she clung to his sweat-glazed body, arching up, slam-ming into every thrust. She couldn't stop herself from crying out his name as they shattered together into a million pieces.

She came back to earth with a thud. She'd done it. She'd done the worst thing she could possibly do. And she wasn't sorry.

Defiant, suffused with the warmth and sweet buzz of afterglow, she held on tight. She buried her head in Ned's shoulder, trying to figure out some way to hold on to this feeling.

Somehow, she knew in her heart nothing would ever be the same.

NED BEGAN TO RECOVER his sanity about ten minutes after he'd had the most mind-blowing sex of his life. They were still rammed into the stairs, him on the bottom and Rose cradled next to him, with their clothes and belongings scattered around like the aftermath of a hurricane.

Well, that pretty much described that, didn't it?

What had he been thinking? If he could blame too much Scotch and her Moulin Rouge number for robbing him of any sense or judgment when he started, he was dead sober now. And she wasn't wearing the outfit.

He opened his eyes, almost afraid to look. Somehow, although he'd managed to get her out of most of it, she still had on those sinful black stockings that covered her up to midthigh. And high-heeled black boots.

The fact that he had made love to her in such a rush on the stairs while she was wearing stockings and boots made it seem all the more bizarre and inappropriate somehow. Not that he was sorry.

That was the weirdest thing. He should've been, but he wasn't sorry at all.

"Rose," he murmured, pressing kisses into her hair. "We should probably move off the staircase at some point."

"Oh, I suppose." Smiling up at him, she shifted away far enough to start pulling together her clothes, and he felt oddly sad to lose the warmth and pressure of her body next to his.

They couldn't stay there forever, although he found himself wishing they could. But real life had a way of intruding, he realized, as he shrugged into his pants and backtracked down enough stairs to collect a missing shoe. Aw, damn. His shirt no longer had any buttons, and he sure as hell wasn't going to go crawling around into the nooks and crannies of the secret staircase to try to find them. He patted the pocket of his jacket.

"Rose? I've got your glasses."

"Oh, thanks." She had her ruffled panties back on—Lord, he loved those things—and she was fastening herself back into her corset. She left it partially unhooked, her pale, luscious breasts mostly uncovered behind the gaping red velvet, as she took the wire-rims from him.

His mouth watered all over again. Was there any way to convince her to go for another round right here on the stairs?

Either she was psychic or the hunger on his face was easy to read. "I think we're pretty close to the top of the stairs," she said in a husky whisper. "I'll race you."

And she took off, juggling her skirt and glasses and his other shoe. All he could do was bring up the rear.

Almost at the very top of the secret staircase, Rose was waiting next to a small door with an antique glass knob. Ned was beginning to wonder if White Rabbits and Cheshire Cats would be on the other side, but he figured it probably didn't matter at this point. It could be the Spanish Inquisition and he'd still follow Rose without a whimper. He ducked his head and slipped through the door.

Judging by the arching open beams overhead, they appeared to be in the attic of the Inn, divided into a warren of smaller rooms and corridors. There were enough windows, plus lots of stars and a full moon, to see fairly well. Although it was breezy and a bit chilly up there, he didn't hear voices or see anyone, although he did spy some leftover furniture and trunks he could only assume came from a part of the Inn's notorious past.

After squeezing through another even smaller door and several odd passages, Rose led him to what looked like a closet tucked under the eaves in the attic.

She looked almost shy when she gestured to the door and said, "Go ahead. Go in."

He was all out of the ability to be surprised when it came to Rose, but he did find this place interesting. As Rose switched on a small lamp, he could see that it really was no bigger than a large closet, full of books and videos and DVDs, as well as a laptop computer, a television, and a VCR, all crammed onto haphazard, slapped-together shelves fashioned out of cement blocks, wooden crates, and random slabs of wood. Nothing appeared to be connected to anything—no wires, no plugs—but she had power somehow, because the lamp worked, and the VCR was flashing the time—1:47. Late.

There were no decorations, no knickknacks, but a pair of chipped porcelain bookends and a deep-garnet

chenille afghan tossed across the only piece of furniture, a soft, dusty-pink chaise longue. It was missing
one of its legs, but had been propped up on a stack of
books. Idly, he pulled a couple of video boxes off the
shelf. *The Godfather* and *Gone With the Wind*.

It reminded him of his dorm room in college, but
what was it? Her hideaway from whatever job she held
at the hotel? Did anybody know she was packing
books and videos into a room in the attic? Not to mention tapping into the electricity. There were no clothes
except for the lingerie he'd seen her in before and his
shirt, no sink, no refrigerator, so she couldn't live here.
Could she?

"What is this place, Rose?"

She lifted her shoulders in a small shrug. "My garret,
if you want to call it that. My little nest."

"Well, it's cute, but...it's kind of odd, I think," he
said softly. "You've got this place with all your stuff in
it, and you can hide out whenever you want, even
sleep here, and you come and go from secret passage-
ways... A little too much *Phantom of the Opera* vibe for
my taste."

"I like it."

"Oh, I like it, too. But, still... Does the hotel manage-
ment know you have this place up here?"

"Well, no," she admitted. She considered the idea
for a moment, chewing on her lip. "Or maybe they do,
actually. Not me specifically, but all of us."

Now he was really confused. "All of you? So your
whole department shares this room for breaks? Something like that?"

"No, no, not like that at all." She began to say something else, broke off, dithered for a minute and then said, "Look, there are some things I have to tell you. Two things. Two big things. I think once I've told you, it would clear all this up, but...maybe confuse things even more. I don't know if I'm allowed to tell you. I've already broken so many rules and I'm not exactly sure why I haven't already been punished." She gazed off into the distance, frowning. "Maybe because everyone is sleeping. Or busy."

Ned raked his hand through his hair. She was making it sound like she was a secret agent or something. Yeah, right. Deep cover at the Inn at Maiden Falls, investigating honeymooners and wedding parties. Well, at least that would explain all the electronics. Rose and her lingerie, running surveillance from the attic. "Rose, you better just tell me whatever it is. It can't be any weirder than what I'm thinking."

"See, I was hoping we could do that later. Because now..."

She smiled, moving closer, laying one small hand on his cheek and threading the other through the open front of his shirt. *Oh, Rose.* His heart beat faster as soon as she touched him, and he couldn't help raising his own hand to the wide gap down the front of her unhooked bustier. Her skin was so soft, and her curves were so tempting. He loved the way her eyes darkened when his hand slipped along the underside of her breast. He pinched her nipple, just a tiny pinch, making it harden and peak, and her lips parted breathlessly.

"I thought," she said slowly, skating one finger along the waistband of his pants, "you and I could curl up on the settee, put in a movie or play some music and..." She took a deep breath, lifting her warm breast more fully into his hand when she exhaled. She inched closer, murmuring, "You would make love to me again. I don't know how long we have before they find out what I've done. And in the meantime...I just want to feel you again. Once. Or twice. As many times as we can."

Oh, God. Did she know what torture this was? It would be so easy to turn off his brain and lose himself in her heat and softness. When he thought about what they'd shared on the stairs... He had to clamp down hard not to rip off her clothes this minute and push her down into that faded pink chaise to see what other trouble they could get into. After all, they'd barely scratched the surface on the stairs.

Ned closed his eyes and took his hand out of her bodice. Broken rules, secrets, hideaways, punishment... It was too freaky to ignore.

So he pulled away and sat on the chaise. By himself. "I think you'd better tell me what it is you have to tell me first. I have to know."

She shook her head, arguing, "If I've learned anything on my unusual journey, it's that a person should do the fun things first and take care of the unpleasant part later. Because you never know what could happen."

"Tell me," he commanded. "You said there were two things. Go with the easy one first."

"I love you," she blurted.

Ned felt as if he'd been punched. He wasn't a person who didn't traded "I love you's" without a whole lot of forethought. Did he love her? He certainly loved making love to her. Did she really love him? How could she know this soon? Besides, even if she did, it did absolutely nothing to explain any of this. "That's the easy one?"

"Not really." She sighed, pacing back and forth in front of him. "It's complicated, I know, because you think we just met. And we did. I mean, a few days ago. But in my heart, we've known each other a very long time."

Okay, so he was hearing "past life" code words. Next she would tell him they were celestial soul mates who'd met in another galaxy or some hocus pocus like that.

She stopped, gazing at him intently. "Ned, I have always loved you. From the very beginning. I mean, even the you that you used to be. Which was a different you in so many ways, but in some ways, the important ways, the same you, too."

Oh, Lord. This just kept getting worse. "The me that I used to be?" he repeated. "When?"

"A long time ago." She knocked a hand against her head. "I didn't put that very well. I told you it was complicated."

"Let's cut it back to the basic idea." He let out a long breath. "You love me."

Her lips curved into a beautiful smile, brimming over with reckless joy. "Uh-huh. I love you. I really like saying that."

"Okay." He wasn't sure where to go with this. He thought for a second, but it still came out a jumble. Maybe that was his problem. Maybe his emotions were always a jumble and it was time to clarify, to figure out what he really wanted. "Rose, I know I have feelings for you, too. I'm not exactly sure what they are, but—"

"Ned, you don't have to—"

But he stood up, taking her shoulders in his hands, feeling the need to share his thoughts on this new breakthrough. Bad move. Bare shoulders. He wheeled away. "I'm not sure, but you have to understand, I think my confusion is more my problem than yours." He paused, frowning. "I think I'm discovering that I have always kind of bottled up my feelings, so maybe I don't know if I love you. I could, but I don't know. Does that make sense?

"Of course it makes sense, but..." Rose huddled on the settee. Idly she began to untie her boots. He could tell by the way she ripped out the laces that she wasn't happy with his reaction to her news. "Ned, I didn't say that I loved you just to get you to tell me you love me, too. I mean, you do. But you can discover that in your own time."

His mouth dropped open. "How can you be sure if I'*m* not sure?"

"Oh, that's easy." She tossed a boot across the room. "It's in your kiss. I can taste it every time you kiss me."

"Aw, Rose, what am I going to do with you?" He joined her on the chaise, watching as she rolled off her stockings and stretched out her legs. She thought there was some imprint of love in his kiss? That was sweet, but hardly reliable. She might as well read it in tea leaves. "You're the most bizarre woman I ever met. In a good way. Mostly. I think." He was just so tired of fighting it. It was late, he'd had too much to drink hours ago, maybe he even had a hangover. This was not the time for deep thinking. "So what was the other thing?"

"Oh." She sighed. "That one."

"Well? We've established that you love me, and that's the easy one." He was actually getting used to the idea that Rose loved him, which was pretty scary in itself. "But what's the hard one?"

"This is going to be tough," she hedged. She took his hand between both of hers. "I'm going to need a leap of faith here. So I need you to trust me."

"I'm here, aren't I?" he asked with only a touch of irony.

"I know you trust me, Ned. I know who you are, and you would never make love to a woman you didn't trust. And that's why I'm going to tell you. Because you deserve to know." She took another deep breath, exhaled, and gazed straight down at their linked hands. "I'm a ghost."

The words didn't process for several minutes. A ghost? Like Casper. Like *Ghostbusters.* Except...there was no such thing. Maybe she meant she was a shadow of her former self. Maybe she meant she was a ghost writer. Maybe...

"When you say *ghost,*" he began, pulling his hand away, "how do you define that?"

"Exactly the same way you do, I think," she said logically. "Spectral being. Poltergeist. Boo! Once alive, now dead. Haunting my former abode until my spirit can pass over. That kind of thing."

He dropped his head into his hands. "I don't believe this."

"How do you think I appear and disappear the way I do? Why do you think I wear lingerie from 1895?" she demanded. "Maybe because I'm *from* 1895?"

This was so much worse than he thought. "Rose, it can't be," he said softly. "I know you believe it, but—"

"It's true, Ned. I know you're aware this place is haunted, because I heard you ask the waitress about it." Rose turned to him, sounding very self-righteous and haughty for someone wearing nothing but a pair of ruffled black underpants and a half-undone red bustier. "The Inn was a bordello back then, back in 1895. Miss Arlotta and all her girls, plus Judge Hangen, Miss Arlotta's beau who'd stopped by that night, died the same night, on a Sunday in June, 1895. I was among them."

"So you're not just a ghost, but the ghost of a dead hooker?" he asked derisively.

"If you want to put it that way." She lifted her chin. "I planned to become a harlot, but I never quite got there because the gas leak occurred on my first night. I was supposed to begin my life as a scarlet woman the very next day, but none of us made it to the next day. So I never did ply the trade, if that's what you're asking. I can understand how it might bother you if you thought I really was a soiled dove, but—"

"It's fine, Rose, really." He had to hand it to her. She certainly had created a whole dossier for her delusion, hadn't she?

"You're sure it doesn't bother you that I was a harlot, however briefly?" she asked doubtfully.

"I'm sure."

"Good. Because that isn't the worst part."

He felt as if the sky were falling in big chunks on his head. "No? There's more?"

"I'm afraid that all of us here, Miss Arlotta and her girls, have been assigned spectral duty, if you want to put it that way, for very specific reasons." She bit her lip. "Since Miss Arlotta ran a house of ill repute, where gentlemen were encouraged to cheat on their wives, we are now supposed to be offering some kind of compensation by making sure that the couples who stay here enjoy total and complete marital bliss. We're honeymoon helpers, you see."

"No," he said, shaking his head, "I don't see."

"Well, that's why I'm in so much trouble. I was assigned to help you and the odious Vanessa," she explained. She reached out to touch his hair. "But I really like you. I love you, Ned. And I think Vanessa stinks." Now she began to sound indignant. "Miss Arlotta and the Judge...well, I don't care how they punish me, I am not going to help Vanessa keep you. That's just wrong."

"Rose, what exactly did you do?" he inquired carefully. If she thought she was entitled to pull anything she wanted to keep Vanessa away from him, what would that entail? Just how off the hook was she?

"I didn't do anything. Although they thought I got her drunk the night of your rehearsal dinner and they actually gave me a gold star for that, as if I were trying to get you two together." She rolled her eyes. "Like I would do that!"

Ned swallowed. He remembered now that there had been cell phone and purse problems, and a few other odd things driving Vanessa crazy at that dinner. It was certainly possible that Rose had had a hand in those mishaps. And not a ghostly hand. Just a devious little dirty trickster's.

Did Rose really think she was on a mission to interfere in people's honeymoons? Specifically his? As he looked around at her hiding place, his brain whirled with terrible thoughts. Was she homeless and a squatter at the hotel? As well as a thief? She'd probably lifted most of this stuff from hotel guests, since she obviously had a master key.

Oh, God. This was bad. And yet he still found himself wanting to protect her.

"Rose," he said gently, "I think you're having some problems telling reality from fantasy. I think you need help."

"Oh, Ned, don't be silly. I don't need that kind of help. But I am going to need help when Miss Arlotta finds out what I've done. Especially the sex part." She sighed. "We are strictly forbidden from sleeping with our grooms. Or anybody else for that matter. She hit the roof when I so much as kissed you, so if she finds out that I slept with you... Oh, heavens. I may be banished to a corner of the attic for eternity. Well, it was worth it." She gave him that smoky, sexy gaze that made his pulse jump. Even now, even when he was pretty sure she was delusional, she still had the power to reel him in. "I'd do it again in a minute."

She stopped in her tracks. "Oh, I just remembered. The wine cellar. I left Lemon Chiffon—the real stripper for your party—locked in the wine cellar so I could take her place. Somebody needs to get her out of there."

She did *what?* Ned felt like there ought to be a big black hole in the floor that he could just fall into. It now appeared he'd had sex with a crazy woman. Worse yet, he'd fallen in love with a crazy woman. *Good news, Rose. I'm now sure I love you. But the bad news is, I'm also sure you're out of your mind.*

"Rose, my aunt is a psychologist," he tried quickly. "I really think you should talk to her. She's very nice, and I know you'll like her. Because this isn't good, Rose, setting up camp in a hotel to spy on people, stealing from the guests, locking strippers in wine cellars and breaking into guys' rooms and getting in bed with them. I know you meant well, but you have to see that this is destructive behavior, okay?"

"I told you, Ned, I don't need that kind of help."

But he could see from the look on her face—pity, dismay, distress—that she'd figured out he didn't believe her and he probably never would. "Don't worry, Rose," he said in his most persuasive voice, "we'll get help. And I'll be with you every step of the way. I'm not letting go just because you have a small problem."

"Oh. All right. I see what you mean." She sounded flat and unemotional now, and he didn't trust the change in tone. "Of course I'll go see your aunt with you. Just let me change my clothes."

She stepped behind him, back to the bookshelves, and he wondered what she was up to. But he didn't have time to figure it out.

The next thing he knew, he heard a sort of a sizzle, felt a sharp pain on his shoulder, then the lights went out and he pitched into total darkness.

9

ROSEBUD WAS in a very bad mood.

That was partly because the man she loved thought she was a lunatic, partly because she'd slept with a man for the first time in forever and it was beyond incredible and now she was doomed never to have sex ever again, and partly because even though she really cared about Ned, she'd found it necessary to zap him unconscious. Life just wasn't fair.

The first thing she did was switch herself back into her regular clothes. She had to have help, and she didn't want any of the other girls to get even a hint of how much she'd been up to in the last forty-eight hours. Different clothes—different from the ones they'd seen her in all these years—would be a major clue that dramatic events had been happening. Of course, since the outgrowth of those forty-eight hours was an unconscious man on the floor of her hidden room and *he* was what she needed help with, somebody was going to know something very soon, anyway.

"My stars. I am in such trouble," she said grimly. She would be walking a tightrope between deception and discovery.

After slipping back into her bloomers and camisole and putting on her spectacles, she scurried down to the first floor to look for one of the other girls. Lavender was her best bet, she figured, since she had a brain and might be willing to keep her mouth shut. But really, she'd have to take whoever she could get at this point.

She wafted quickly in and out of the lobby, not seeing anyone useful, adding a swoop around the historical parlor while she was down there. No one.

Damnation.

She headed for the roof. If only Sunshine or Belle were still here. They had been loyal friends with excellent talents. She knew they would've helped her in a minute, and would never breathe a word to Miss Arlotta. But they'd both played by the rules, hadn't they? They'd collected all their gold stars and their notches in the Bedpost Book, and ascended to the Big Picnic in the Sky. Unlike some ghost hookers she could think of. Herself, for example.

"Well, Rosebud," she muttered to herself, "you really did it this time. You broke all the rules, you fell in love, and you were stupid enough to tell him the truth. Fat lot you've learned in 109 years."

The really sad thing was that the last man who'd seduced and betrayed her was also a Mulgrew. What was it about that family?

"Oh, sure. Seduced and betrayed." She planted her hands on her hips. "Be honest, Rosebud. Maybe Edmund was a cad, but not Ned. The seducer this time was you, missy. You knew you couldn't have him and you did it, anyway. You're a ghost, you idiot! What did you think you were going to do with a mortal man?"

Funny how Miss Arlotta's golden rules were starting

to sound pretty smart. All this time, she'd thought those rules were for the guests' protection. Not hers.

"Rosebud?" somebody asked behind her in a very cranky tone. "Are you carrying on a conversation all by your lonesome, girl? What are you, tetched?"

That whiny tone could only be Flo. Rosebud turned. Yep. The Queen of Bad Moods had arrived. "Yes, Flo, some people do think I'm touched in the head. Why do you ask?"

"I don't know what you're doing floating around at this time of night," Flo said sourly. "I'd be fast asleep in my bed if I could. But I'm afraid even the smallest nap has been denied me because of the infernal pain I suffer from this corset. I could tear that Mimi's hair out by the roots for never coming to loosen my knots and forcing me to pass into eternity this way."

As if she hadn't heard that story ten thousand times. Twenty thousand. Rosebud turned back to the wrought-iron rail around the roof, gazing off into the distance at the Falls. She could hear the clean, cool rush of water from here. Maybe if she concentrated, the sound of the Falls would drown out Flo and her corset complaints.

"Hmph," Flo sniffed, giving Rosebud the fish-eye. "I declare, Rosebud, you're not wearing yours. Your corset. What have you done?"

She glanced down. *Uh-oh.* When she'd redressed, she'd put on her usual camisole with the rosebud embroidery and her frilly bloomers, but she'd forgotten the stupid corset. But that gave her an idea. Hmmm... She looked back. How strong was Flo, anyway?

"Flo, I've discovered something regarding our

ghostly clothing that I think will be of special interest to you," she said sweetly. "I think you and I might be able to make a deal here."

"What kind of deal?"

"I can help you loosen your knots. Or take the blasted thing off completely if you want to." She took Flo's arm. "After all this time, imagine what it would feel like to be pinched and confined no longer. Just imagine, Flo."

"You saying you know how to do that?" the other ghost asked suspiciously.

"I'm not wearing mine, am I? How do you think I did that?" Rosebud did a little twirl. "You know every girl has her talents. But I've discovered another talent. How to change clothes."

"And you'd share this trick with me?"

"Yes, I would." She crossed her arms over her chest. "If you do one little favor for me."

"What favor would that be?" Flo inquired, narrowing her eyes.

"I have a problem," Rosebud said flat out. "I made a mistake."

She wasn't at all sure she could trust Flo, but sometimes you had to make that leap of faith. Even if Ned wouldn't. But she wasn't going to dwell on that.

She explained, "It's really very easy. I need you to help me transport someone who is too heavy for me to carry by myself. And you have to promise not to say anything to Miss Arlotta or anyone else." She made a twisting motion, like she was turning a key in her lips. "Do we have a deal?"

"All righty." Flo nodded. "But you have to release me from my durn corset first."

She'd anticipated that one. Flo wasn't going to be much help toting men around if she was still imprisoned in her too-tight corset, anyway. "All right. Here's what you do. First, you have to make yourself visible. How good are you at that?"

"I'm poor at it. It's agin the rules," Flo retorted. "Why should I do that?"

"Well, do it now. It's the only way. Fully three-dimensional. Concentrate."

Flo flickered into view, faded and indistinct.

"I don't know if it'll work, as wobbly as you are," Rosebud critiqued. "But I guess we'll have to try. Hold yourself as visible as possible. Focus on filling in every detail."

But nothing happened. Flo was the worst materializer she'd ever seen. She had no idea if it would work, but she used her own powers to help fill in Flo's dots. "That's better," she said out loud. "Close your eyes, Flo."

Rosebud did the same, made herself completely visible and concentrated on loosening the stupid knots.

"Oh, my stars in the morning!" Flo gasped, her eyes popping open. "I felt 'em comin' loose!"

"Shut your eyes!" Rosebud ordered. As soon as they were both working on it, the knots slowly disappeared, the laces untied, and the corset eased around Flo's matronly middle.

"I could kiss you!" the older ghost exclaimed.

"No need. Come on. We have work to do."

Rosebud grabbed Flo's hand and dragged her along

behind her as she flew back down to the attic. "You're going to see my hideaway, Flo. My room, where nobody knows I go when I want to be alone. It's none of your business and you can just forget you saw it as soon as we leave, okay?"

"Why would you want a hidey-hole, Rosebud? Who do you think you are, Jesse James?"

Rosebud ignored her. "You will also notice there is an unconscious man on the floor. We need to move him back to his room, that's all."

Flo's eyes grew round. "Who is he?" She stooped and poked at Ned's side. "Did you kill him?"

"No, of course I didn't kill him," Rosebud snapped. "I had to give him a small shock, that's all. Enough to knock him out and I hope give him about forty-eight hours of memory loss. But he'll be fine." Her gaze softened as she hitched Ned up by the shoulders and Flo took his feet. "Be gentle, all right?"

"Where we goin', Rosebud?" Flo asked in a quavery voice. "Are we vergin' on trouble for this?"

"Is there a rule against moving unconscious men, Flo? No! So why should you get in trouble?" She backed up slowly, heading for the stairs. She'd never tried to carry a mortal through ceilings or floorboards, so she figured the staircase was the best choice. Thank goodness Ned's room was on the third floor, not too far from the secret passage, and no one saw the prone man hanging in the air all by himself, hauled along by invisible harlots.

"Wasn't this your room, Rosebud?" Flo asked when they finally had him downstairs and inside his room.

"I don't reckon I've been in here since the gas leak in '95."

"Yes, it was my room." She pulled the sheets up over Ned, even though it seemed silly to put him in bed wearing an open shirt, a jacket, trousers and shoes. But she hadn't trusted herself to undress him. Not even a little.

"With any luck," she said out loud, "he'll remember the bachelor party, think he'd had too much to drink, and block out the rest of it entirely."

That would mean blocking out making love to her. She shivered. She didn't care what anyone did to her, she would never forget it. But she couldn't speak for him, could she?

"Are we done then?" Flo asked in her usual vinegary tone. "He was a heavy son of a gun and I think I put out my back."

"Yes, you're done. Go. Please. But remember, not a word," Rosebud instructed. "Or I'll put your corset back the way it was!"

She didn't really think she could do that, but she hoped the warning would keep Flo's mouth securely shut. That seemed like a pipe dream, now that she thought about it more clearly. Flo was too crotchety to keep a promise for its own sake.

"Even if she blabs to every person she knows, it's not like this can get any worse," Rosebud said gloomily. "I'm already stuck somewhere nastier than any of Dante's Circles of Hell."

She turned back to Ned. He looked as if he were sleeping peacefully. But she knew she'd zapped him with an electric shock, even if it wasn't obvious at first glance.

"You'd better be all right." She set a hand on his forehead. He was warm, not hot, and clearly breathing. He was okay, wasn't he? "I'm sorry, Ned. You see, I make terrible decisions when I go too quickly. I've been impetuous since the day I was born, and it has always gotten me into trouble."

She bit her lip, bending over him, pulling the sheet up to his chin, peeling it back an inch or two, wanting so badly to touch him, but not trusting herself.

After dithering there for a moment, she knew she had to go. Softly she whispered, "I still love you." She leaned over and quickly kissed him on the cheek. "I didn't mean to hurt you. I hope you're okay."

And then she backed out of his room before she forgot herself and lay down beside him again.

Friday morning

NED AWOKE to the mother of all headaches.

"Oh, my God. What did I do last night?" he mumbled, sitting up, holding his head to stop the room from whirling around like that. "Where am I?"

His own hotel room? He pulled back the sheets. And he was wearing the clothes he'd had on last night, except there were now no buttons on his shirt. And he had his shoes on. In bed.

The first thing he did was kick off the shoes. He got up and stumbled into the bathroom for a drink of water. He felt like a truck had run over him. A big truck.

Why wasn't his brain working at all? He could barely remember his name, let alone where he'd been.

"Okay, time to retrace my steps," he decided.

He found his PDA on the dresser and turned it on. He was a schedule maker by nature, so his handheld computer should tell him the bare bones of what he'd been doing. Ah. Last night had been the bachelor party, of course, so that explained part of it. Drinking, cigars, a stripper.

"Rose," he said darkly. He stood up so fast the room started to spin again.

Things were coming back in bits and pieces now. Rose. She'd been in his room twice. He'd woken up with her yesterday morning. Or the day before? He couldn't remember. And then last night, she'd popped out of the cake.

He started to swear, the most vicious, foul things he could think of, as the memories played in vivid color in his brain. The secret staircase. Making love to Rose like a wild man. And then, she'd taken him to some little room.

"Like her lair," he spit out. "Like she thinks she's a comic book crime fighter. But, no. Crime fighter isn't wacky enough. This one thinks she's a ghost."

It would've been funny if it weren't so sad. "It would've been sad if she hadn't tasered me," he said with contempt. That was the only thing that made sense to explain why he'd felt a shock and passed out. *Tasered* him! And to think he'd told Chris not to call her *the crazy chick.* "The crazy chick used a stun gun on me!"

He picked up the phone, punching in the number for

the hotel manager, ready to give somebody an earful about the potentially psychopathic stalker who was also a squatter in their attic. But then he hung up it before anyone answered.

"She's not a psychopath," he realized. "She may be a little crazy—okay, a lot crazy—but she's not that over the edge." Besides, who would believe his story? "Even I wouldn't believe that story."

Like how exactly he'd gotten back from this supposed lair in the attic to his own room. Was a woman barely over five feet tall who weighed about a hundred pounds going to casually toss him in a laundry cart and wheel him through three tiny doors and down a set of rickety, narrow stairs? Yeah, right.

Besides, he'd made love to her. On those stairs! And he was supposed to marry somebody else tonight. Tonight!

Ned lifted a hand to his forehead. "Oh, God. Vanessa."

No matter what else he did, he had to get to Vanessa. He had to break it off.

He dialed her room, but there was no answer. She was probably out attending to the last-minute wedding details she was so obsessed with. "I can't call off a wedding with a note or voice mail," he muttered helplessly. But he did call back and leave a message. "Vanessa, it's Ned. I really need to speak with you as soon as possible. Call me, please?"

She was probably going to know what was up with that, anyway. The last time he'd seen her, he was supposed to be sleeping on some kind of decision about them. Vanessa wasn't stupid. She knew he was already backtracking. But surely she wouldn't want to marry him if she knew he was fresh off an erotic staircase encounter with a woman who was so nutty she thought she was a ghost?

Next he tried his mother. He thought he could really use some advice from her. Or maybe some help telling Vanessa he wasn't going to marry her. Not in.

Next choice was Aunt Edwina. At least she knew how to deal with crazy people. And thank God she answered the phone.

"Aunt Win, I need to see you right away. I need your help. Bad."

"Ned, you sound terrible. Are you okay?"

"No, I'm not. Can you meet me downstairs?" he asked with as much urgency as he could muster when his head was pounding like that. "There's this little red room off the main lobby. It's kind of private. I think they call it the historical parlor. Meet me there in five minutes, okay?"

He took the quickest shower in the history of the universe and changed into jeans and a T-shirt. Given that one of his shirts had no buttons and another had gone missing entirely, he was running out of dress shirts.

When he got to the red parlor, his aunt was already there.

"Hi, sweetie," she announced, turning to give him a kiss. "I didn't know this parlor was here. But what a good idea. The history of this place is fascinating, isn't it?"

"Yeah, it's a real hoot."

"Okay." She gave him a speculative glance. "I hear your bachelor party got pretty exciting last night."

"What did you hear?" he asked slowly.

"Well, Jerry was the only one of the owners actually on the premises, so they contacted him about the stripper they found locked in the wine cellar." Her eyes held a curious light. "I guess you had an impostor stripper?"

Ned looked at the floor. "Oh, really?"

So Rose really had locked the stripper in the wine cellar. *Rose, Rose, what am I going to do with you?*

"I also heard the lights went out." She paused. "And you disappeared during the blackout, as did the impostor stripper. There was speculation you'd left together, since apparently some amazing chemistry was observed between you while she was giving you a lap dance to end all lap dances." Dryly she added, "That I got from Jerry himself, who came late to the party but got an eyeful."

There was an overstuffed Victorian arm chair in the parlor, and Ned sunk into it even though it was too small for him. He just needed to sit down. "What am I going to do, Aunt Win? My life is a shambles."

"So that's what you wanted to talk to me about?" She smiled. "Professionally or personally? I guess it doesn't matter. That's easy, Ned. As either your aunt or your shrink I'd tell you the same thing. Follow your heart. You're a great guy and a wonderful person. You won't make the wrong choice. And whatever you choose, you know Uncle Jerry and I will always be on your side."

He stared at the desk in front of him, unwilling to meet her eyes.

She said softly, "Okay, if you need me to spell it out,

I will. If you ask me, it's past time to call off this wedding."

"Oh, the wedding. I already came to that conclusion, thank you. I tried first thing this morning. I'll tell her as soon as I can find her." He glanced up, joking, "Maybe I should look on the bright side. Maybe the reason I can't find her is that she already dumped me and left the hotel."

She moved in closer. "Interesting. So if you didn't want to talk to me about Vanessa, what is it? Don't tell me it's the stripper. You met her last night and fell madly in love? This is getting good, Ned! Surprising coming from you, but fascinating. And why did she lock the other one in the cellar? Professional jealousy or something?"

"I met her a few nights ago. She's not really a stripper, Aunt Win. It's worse than that." He leaned over the desk and its display of bordello memorabilia, propping his head on one arm. "At first she told me she was a hotel maid. Then she jumped out of my cake. And last night..." He hesitated. Even telling someone he knew would never judge him, it still sounded ridiculous. "She said she's a ghost."

"Oh. Well, that's entertaining."

"You could at least take it a little bit seriously. I'm in agony here!" he protested. "When I told her I didn't believe she was a ghost, I think she zapped me with a stun gun and dragged me back to my hotel room. Plus she definitely locked the real stripper in the wine cellar. That is not normal behavior. She thinks it's part and parcel of being a ghost. Like the ghostly mischief she gets into or something."

His aunt chewed her lip absently, staring into space over his head. "So, she thinks she's a ghost in this hotel? I suppose one option would be to believe her."

"Huh?"

"'There are more things in heaven and earth, Horatio, than are dreamt of in your philosophy,'" she quoted. At his blank look, she added, "You know, from *Hamlet*. Shakespeare?"

"You'll forgive me if I don't find it all that persuasive. Shakespeare's been dead a long time."

"So has your girlfriend, if she's telling the truth," she said with a mischievous grin. "I know it sounds crazy, Ned, but seriously, there are a lot of strange things that go on in this hotel. Jerry has told me some of the stories, and I was just reading up before you got here. Did you know the place was a bordello, and some people believe that the ghosts of old hookers haunt the Inn, making sure that honeymooners have a really good time while they're here?"

"That's just what she said," he groaned. "She must've read the materials down here." He began flipping open the books in front of him. "See, right here it says the madam was named Miss Arlotta. She said that, too. And she said..."

But he stopped in midsentence. The page he'd turned to was an old-time photo, a tintype or a daguerreotype of the ladies who had once worked here, posing in this very parlor in their lingerie. And in the back row, standing a bit separate from the others, was Rose. Same camisole with embroidery around the neckline, same bloomers, same corset cinching in her waist. He traced a finger over the picture. Same stubborn chin, same soft curls, same delicious breasts tipping over the top of her tiny little shirt...

Ned didn't know if he trusted his eyes. Especially not when everything in the room was twirling like a tilted carousel. "Aunt Win, you need to look at this. In the back row, on the end, the small brunette with the ringlets. That's her."

She followed the legend with her finger. "Rosebud? She's your girl?"

"She said her name was Rose. But this can't be." Ned stood up, pounding a fist into the desk, making the books jump. "There are no such things as ghosts. I know that. It seems more likely that my girl, Rose, saw this picture, too, and dressed like it as part of her delusion. She lives in this hotel, Aunt Win, like some Phantom of the Opera wannabe, running around playing dirty tricks on people, stealing stuff from guests and the hotel. And locking strippers in the wine cellar."

"And apparently sleeping with you."

A long pause hung there between them. "I didn't say I slept with her."

"You didn't have to." She patted him on the arm. "Okay, Ned. Seriously now. Do I think it's likely that she's a ghost? No, I don't. Do I think there's a happy ending for this, whether she is or not? I have no idea."

"I'm not asking about happy endings," he insisted. "I'm asking about how to handle her now. She may be crazy, but..." He jammed his hand through his hair, as if pulling his hair out by the roots would make sense come back to his brain. "But I still care about her. I still want her. How can that be?"

"If you really do care for her, then she's a lucky girl." She put an arm around him. "Sweetie, I think the most logical explanation is that she's a perfectly ordinary, maybe even borderline neurotic woman, who's formed an attachment to you. You know, like a crush. It's easy for that kind of thing to happen." She gave him an apologetic shrug. "You're kind of a hunk."

"A perfectly ordinary, borderline neurotic woman... I wish that were true," he lamented. "It would make life so much easier."

His aunt just laughed at that one. "The whole point is not to be easy, but to be difficult, complicated, intriguing and dramatic. Caught your attention, didn't it? I'm starting to wonder if this woman isn't someone you dated a few times back in 1997 or something and you've completely forgotten about. Given your dating history, it's entirely possible. And that would explain why and when she formed the fixation."

"Well, she did say she'd been in love with me for a long time. Something about the me that I used to be. It was very strange," he reflected.

"Exactly. So she has this crush on you, she hears you're getting married, and she comes here determined to break up your engagement." She shook her head. "And you were willing and able to jump on any old excuse to do exactly that because you didn't want to get married in the first place. An excuse like magical ghost hookers haunting an old bordello is certainly different, Ned. You have to give her credit for creativity."

"So you think I fell for her because of the timing, as an excuse not to think about the wedding, or maybe to get out of the wedding?" he asked, confused.

"Let me put it this way, sweetie," his aunt told him fondly, kissing him on the cheek on her way out of the parlor. "I think chances are good that if you march yourself up to Vanessa right this minute and tell her the engagement and the wedding are kaput, your fascination for Little Rosebud, the combination stripper, ghost hooker and Phantom of the Opera, will magically disappear."

It sounded so easy. So why couldn't he take his eyes off that picture? Why was Rosebud, the fallen maiden from 1895, a dead ringer for his Rose?

Why couldn't he stop thinking about what it was like when they made love on the stairs? That was real, tangible, cataclysmic, not some figment of his imagination.

You do love me, Ned. It's in your kiss. I can taste it every time you kiss me.

"Where are you, Rose?" he asked out loud. "At the moment, I don't care if you're someone I slept with at a frat party in 1994, a Fatal Attraction, or the Ghost of Christmas Past. I want to see you. I need to touch you."

He crossed to the bookshelf, and he began pulling off volumes one and two at a time. One of them had to work. He was going to find the secret passageway. And find Rose's lair.

10

Friday afternoon

"ROSEBUD, it's for your own good, sugar," Glory told her from where she was sitting on top of the banded trunk. Rosebud pounded her fist against the lid from inside, but Glory ignored her. "Great day in the mornin', you sure can cause a ruckus."

"Glory, let me out. Please?" she begged. "Des, are you still there, too? Can you get me out?"

"Heck, no," Desdemoaner said mournfully, pulling out the word "no" to about six syllables. "I don't want Miss Arlotta after my tail, too. Me and Glory's just off the black mark list after dropping a few toys in Wee Willie's room. Should've thought of that right off. If his willie is too wee, why, give him a bigger one, even if it is pink and plastic."

"I'm thrilled for you that your assignment worked out so well," Rosebud snapped with a whole lot of aggravation. "But mine didn't. And it's important that I get out of here. I think Ned may still be getting married tonight, which is a travesty! I have to be there."

"And that's exactly why you're under wraps, hon," Glory reminded her. "Miss Arlotta wants the poor boy to get hitched without you gitting in the middle of it. She says once he's proper married and sent on his way, then it's safe to let you out."

"If I vere you, Rosebud," the Countess contributed in her cartoon villain accent, "I vould spend my time in ze trunk zinking up vays to defend myself. Az zoon az your groom flies de coop viz his bride, ve all know Miss Arlotta vill hev your head on ze silver platter. Ze rumor is zat you had zex viz heem and zen tried to keel him. Very, very naughty, Leetle Rosebud," she finished up in a singsong voice, tapping on Rosebud's trunk in time with her words.

"I didn't try to kill him!" Rosebud slumped to the bottom of the trunk, and her words got muffled down there. "I gave him a small, understated shock, that's all. I'm good with electricity."

That wretched Flo had ratted on her, almost as soon as she'd turned her back. And then Miss Arlotta had really hit the ceiling, furious that Rosebud knew how to fly under the radar so well. Miss A had been completely unaware of the secret room, and that lapse really got under her skin.

"It's not my fault she didn't know about it." Well, actually, it was, but wasn't that the whole point?

Once she'd been informed of its existence, Miss Arlotta had ordered Flo and the Countess to clean out the room completely, with every single book, DVD and video returned to the hotel library, with the exception of *Little Rosebud's Lovers* and *Lady Audley's Secret*, since Rosebud had brought those with her. The lamp, the settee, even the chipped porcelain bookends, were dumped elsewhere in the hotel.

"It's really very distressing," Rosebud maintained from deep inside the trunk.

Miss Arlotta also knew about the bachelor party and her Moulin Rouge act, and Mimi was furious that

Rosebud had copied her Folies Bergere song. "Pish tosh! She doesn't own it," Rosebud muttered.

At this point, Rosebud wasn't sure anyone knew about the s-e-x and she didn't want to even think about the word in case someone had been practicing mind reading. They were all aware that Ned had been seen lying on the floor of her secret room, although no one knew what was wrong with him or why he was passed out or what had led to that curious turn of events. Miss Arlotta sent Mimi to check on him, and she reported back that she'd seen him in the historic parlor pulling books off shelves and that he looked "magnifique!"

"I wonder what he was doing in the parlor," Rosebud mused. That seemed odd. But then, why wasn't he canceling his wedding? Did he have no gumption whatsoever? Or just no sense?

Aside from questions about how to play a video, mostly the others seemed curious about how she'd changed her clothes and loosened Flo's corset, and what she and Ned had been up to before he ended up unconscious on her floor. She had no intention of spilling the beans about that.

Overall, Miss Arlotta was furious, railing that there seemed to be a lot of information Rosebud was holding back, and as soon as the boss had a free minute, Rosebud was expected to start coming clean. Special talents, secret rooms, what she was doing with so many videos and DVDs, what had happened between her and Ned when no one was looking…

"There just aren't enough black marks to cover this," Rosebud said grimly as she lay flat across the bottom of the trunk they'd captured her in. All the talents she had, and she couldn't find her way out of one stupid trunk. It was galling.

But then she sat up. Were there truly not enough black marks to cover all her mischief? Interesting.

If she'd already done enough to surpass the black mark possibilities then she was perfectly free to do whatever she wanted, because there was simply no way to punish her any more than they already would based on what she'd already done. At least that sounded plausible.

She started biting her fingernails, each one in sequence. If only she knew more about the possible punishments. Neither Miss Arlotta nor the Judge was ever very specific. Boiled in oil, drawn and quartered, turned into a mouse and doomed to spend eternity looking for spare cheese... Anything was possible.

But whatever it was, she knew she was going to get the maximum based on the s-e-x, even if they never found out about what she'd been up to today before they caught her. She hadn't gone anywhere near Ned, but she'd definitely given Vanessa a few things to think about. Although it was annoying that she'd had to be the one to step in and put a crimp in wedding proceedings that never should've gotten this far. Why couldn't Ned cancel his own wedding?

Rosebud smiled with satisfaction. She might still be a tad miffed at Ned, for thinking she was crazy and wanting her to see a psychiatrist and all, but she had calmed down somewhat. *I know he loves me, not Vanessa, and I know we can find some way to work out the kinks.* Yes, it was a major problem that she happened to live in the spirit world while he was a mortal, but she felt sure there was a way. Maybe she could talk Ned into getting a job here at the Inn, and if the Judge and Miss Arlotta would be reasonable for five seconds, they would let her be in charge of haunting him full-time until he died, and then he could be a ghost, too. See? There was a compromise off the top of her head. Not so hard.

"Really! People can be so inflexible," she grumbled.

Of course, the likelihood that either the Judge or Miss A would be in a conciliatory mood was very, very small. Like, nonexistent. And the likelihood that she would ever see Ned again once they consigned her to whatever punishment they decided upon... She put her hands over her face. Worse than nonexistent.

Suddenly Rosebud sat up in the trunk. If she would never see him again once her sentence was passed, then she'd better make damn sure she saw him before she got to her hearing. Like *now*.

She ran her hands over the inside of the heavy trunk, looking for a crack or a seam. There had to be a way out of here. There had to.

"I'm coming, Ned," she whispered. "I'm coming."

"WHERE THE HELL IS VANESSA?" Ned asked no one in particular. He was running out of time, and he couldn't find the bride.

Every person he asked gave him a different story. First, he heard that Vanessa's high-class wedding planner flown in from New York had tripped and hit her head in the lobby of the Inn, and had been rushed to the nearest ER to check for a concussion, and Vanessa had ridden with her in the ambulance.

Then someone in the sales office told him that neither the florist nor the special caterer had shown up at all, that both had claimed to receive calls canceling their services. So Vanessa was frantically trying to round up flowers somewhere else and harangue the hotel chef to whip up something for her. Although Ned couldn't find her, he did manage to tell the chef and the florist that it wasn't necessary, that yes, the wedding really was canceled.

Now if he could just inform Vanessa.

"What a nightmare," he said fiercely. "You'd think she would get the idea that all this bad karma is happening for a reason."

"Sir? Excuse me? Are you Ned Mulgrew?" a man in a suit asked him.

"Yes. Why?"

"Nice to meet you, Mr. Mulgrew. I'm Joe Bisley, the catering manager. You're the groom in the wedding this evening in the ballroom, right?"

"Yes. Supposedly," he admitted.

"I'm really sorry to have to tell you this, Mr. Mulgrew," the man said reluctantly, "but we've had a slight flood in the ballroom where your reception was supposed to take place, and..."

"A flood? How is that possible?"

"Sprinkler system? Malfunction?" He held up a hand. "We're trying to dry it out as quickly as we can. We're on it, Mr. Mulgrew. But we haven't been able to locate your bride to let her know and we've had some dealings with her earlier in the week, so we're aware that she can be, um, difficult? So we were hoping you might run interference for us."

"Look, don't worry about it. You won't need to dry out the ballroom on our account." Ned fished in his pocket for his wallet and pulled out a hundred. "I haven't been able to locate her, either, but we won't need the ballroom."

"Oh. You've decided to move your reception elsewhere?"

"No. It's, um, off." He gave the poor guy the hundred-dollar bill and sent him back to his wet ballroom.

All these accidents and calamities piling up... It couldn't be coincidence, could it? If he didn't know better, he'd think Rose was behind all of it. Easy enough to make a few phone calls, but flooding the ballroom wasn't that simple. And what about the wedding planner and her concussion? Was Rose capable of staging a slip-and-fall in the hotel lobby without giving away her presence at all?

He made a mental checklist. That cleared the ballroom for the reception, the other room scheduled for the wedding ceremony, the florist and the food. He'd called every guest he knew about to tell them, too. He'd even gone over the merger possibilities with Vanessa's father in the absence of a marriage in the family.

Those were all the bases he knew to cover. He'd been so little involved in the planning that he really didn't have a clue what else to try to cancel.

And where the hell was Vanessa?

"Maybe I'd better check the wine cellar," he said suddenly.

IT HAD GOTTEN VERY QUIET inside the attic. Glory, Desdemoaner, even the Countess, had gotten tired of tormenting her while she was in the trunk. Finally they'd all trundled off. Rosebud knew it was now or never.

"Sunshine," she whispered. "I know you passed over already. I know you're eating fried chicken at the Big Picnic in the Sky this very minute. But if you could see fit to inspire me and help me with wind, I would really appreciate it. I know weather was your special talent and not mine, but I could really use a minor hurricane about now."

And as easily as that, the secret to starting a windstorm flashed into Rosebud's mind.

"Thank you!" She sat up and got to work.

Holding herself very tight, she created the image she wanted, winced, squeezed her eyes shut and waited till the big wooden chest blew apart into bits. Rosebud blinked, glancing around at the splintered slats. "Wow. That was impressive."

But there was no time to crow about her achievement. She had a wedding to get to.

Fueled by fury, she zoomed down the elevator shaft, headed straight for the Fallen Maiden Chapel on the second floor. The hotel frequently used it for weddings, and she knew it was on tap for Ned and Vanessa because she'd read the files in the sales office.

The doors to the chapel were closed, but that didn't even slow her down. She blasted in there like an avenging angel, blowing the doors off, quickly whipping up a howling whirlpool of wind.

It was only after she'd turned over most of the chairs and spun the bride around a few times that she noticed how few people there were in the chapel. There was a minister, the bride and her parents, bridesmaids, and about ten guests. Of course, since she'd brought on her tornado routine, they'd all taken shelter under their chairs, but still...

No groom? No father or mother of the groom? She was trying to figure out what it all meant when Glory, Desdemoaner, Mimi, Flo, Lavender and the Countess all advanced on her in one big battalion of unhappy hookers.

They surrounded her, trapping her. No matter which way she turned, there was a scarlet woman in her face. Before she knew it, they'd tied her up with Flo's old corset strings and towed her back to the attic. It was humiliating. It was beyond upsetting!

"This is really getting old," she cried. "And I didn't even get to see Ned! Couldn't you have waited a few more minutes?"

"You are ze one who make ze grand escape and zen ze tempest," Mimi countered. "Oooh la la! Such a catastrophe!"

"You're giving all of us a bad name," Lavender said with a glare. "No more slipups. We're riding herd till Miss Arlotta and the Judge come in to preside."

"Ve vill be your chury, Leetle Rosebud," the Countess sneered.

"My chury?"

"Jury, sugar," Glory explained. "I'm sorry as all get out, but you're going on trial, hon."

"But I have to know what's going on downstairs," she argued, already fighting against her bonds. "I have to know what happened to Ned!"

THE PLACE WAS A SHAMBLES when Ned walked in.

"Where have you been?" Vanessa cried. She was trying desperately to put her veil to rights. "Never mind. The judge is here, you're here and I'm here and that's all that matters. Let's just get it over with."

"Vanessa," he said firmly. "I've been looking for you all day. I left about fifteen or twenty messages for you, and I talked to both your mother and father. Everyone knows by now that we are not getting married."

"I was at the hospital," she countered. "With my poor wedding planner and her concussion. I didn't have any idea."

But he glanced back at her parents and knew that she knew.

He took her hands and said simply, "I can't marry you. I am in love with someone else."

Vanessa hauled back and slapped him, hard. She sailed straight for the open doorway, not even bothering to look back. "I have never been so glad to leave anywhere in my life!" she wailed. "This place is haunted! By mean, *mean* ghosts!"

Watching her stalk away, with her parents scurrying to keep up, Ned was ashamed, guilty, embarrassed and relieved beyond belief. "It's over," he said with a sigh. "It's finally over."

ROSEBUD TRIED not to shrink. She was not a cowering person by nature, but when she was faced with the full force of imperious Miss Arlotta, the solemn Judge and the jury of her ghostly peers, it was hard not to shrivel up and beg for mercy.

"The list of charges," Judge Hangen announced in his grandest voice, "is long and grievous. Not only did you plot on several occasions to keep a couple apart, breaking rule #1 of the Golden Rules, but it has been brought to our attention that you were visible on numerous occasions breaking rule #2, and you engaged in carnal embrace with a groom under your care, breaking rule #3. Sexual malfeasance of that nature is very, very grave indeed."

At that one, several of her jurors shook their heads, and Glory looked like she might start to cry. You could almost hear the "tsk, tsk" noises.

Rosebud knew it was all over. If they had her dead to rights on the carnal embrace thing, she didn't have anywhere to go but down. *Oh, Lord.* She really wished they'd been clearer about punishments. Her heart began to sink. Could they turn her into a salamander? Bind her, gag her, toss her into the cellar? Or maybe just let the Countess poke her with a sharp stick?

Anything was possible. There was no precedent as far as she knew, because no one had strayed this badly before.

"Given your attempts to separate a bride and groom, excess visualization and, most importantly, sexual malfeasance, we can only conclude that your conduct has been most egregious," the Judge declared.

"And then you also tried to sabotage his wedding ceremony," Miss Arlotta tossed in, sounding really personally peeved and offended, "even after you were warned to stay away, even after we stuck you in a trunk to ensure that very thing, which constitutes willful and flagrant disobedience and flouting of the authority and rules of me, Miss Arlotta, who is in charge here and always has been. That, Rosebud, is so bad there isn't even a rule for it."

"I know I wasn't supposed to, but I love him!" Rosebud cried. "I couldn't help it! What was I supposed to do, let him marry a twit he didn't love? He loves me!"

She noticed at that point that the room had gone very still. She swallowed. "I love him," she said again.

"And if you think that helps your case, you are sadly mistaken," Miss Arlotta said grimly.

"Enough." The Judge pounded his gavel. "Members of the Council, you've heard the charges, and you have also heard that the defendant did not offer much in the way of mitigating factors except that she allegedly has amorous feelings for this mortal groom. So I invite you to retreat to discuss a verdict. Miss Arlotta, when you're ready, you go right ahead and do your worst."

It seemed to take forever for all of them to huddle together to discuss her punishment. She saw frowns and glowers, she saw disagreements among them over what the best course of action was, and she saw the Countess jabbering on and on, which couldn't be good. If the Countess had any sway, Rosebud knew she would be pushing rocks up the stairs with her nose for the rest of eternity.

And why was it taking so long? They all knew what she'd done. There wasn't a bit of disagreement about that, and she hadn't even tried to defend herself. Well, except for that bit about falling in love with a mortal, which was really more of a confession than a defense. But she didn't point that out. She tried to wait as patiently as she could, which was, as it happened, not at all patient.

All she knew was that the man she loved was missing and unaccounted for and she wanted to find him, damn it. "Nobody ever cares what I think or listens to me," she said heatedly from her corner of the attic.

The Judge and Desdemoaner looked up from what they were doing to glance over her way when she said that. But after a few raised eyebrows, they went right back to their deliberations. The Countess cried, "Nyet! Zis vill not do!" but the Judge wagged a finger at her and she quieted down.

Hmmm... If the Countess didn't like it, it had to be good news.

Finally, after Rosebud had decided she was going to turn into a statue if they didn't come back soon, Miss Arlotta swept around from behind the big, imposing desk and headed directly for her.

"Stand here and take your punishment," Miss Arlotta commanded. She pointed to a spot about a foot in front of her.

Quavering a little, Rosebud did as she was told.

"Rosebud, you have committed severe and terrible offenses." She shook her platinum curls sadly. "I never did think you would fit in here. Not for a minute. And I know you were caught in with the rest of us when you had not actually plied our trade and I know you chafed at being subject to our restrictions. But, Rosebud, you gotta play the hand you're dealt. Instead you tried to tilt the table and knock all the cards on the floor. And that ain't right."

Whispers of agreement hissed from the assembly of soiled doves. Rosebud saw the Countess nod vigorously, and Flo press her lips into a thin line of disapproval.

"Therefore," the madam continued, "it is the decision of the Council that based on the offenses committed and the lack of remorse shown by Rosebud that we have no choice but to sentence you to the worst punishment we can think of."

Rosebud's heart dropped to her knees. She would

never see Ned again. She would never see the sun again.

But there was a soft smile on Glory's face, Des looked like she might be stifling a giggle, and the Judge...the grand and imposing Judge, who wasn't known to even attempt a smile, winked at her. He *winked* at her! What could that mean?

"I'm sorry, Rosebud," the boss proclaimed. "We did our level best to come up with a punishment that would fit your crime, and seein' as how the Judge and me, we got a free hand and a whole lot of power to do whatever we like, we came up with something kinda unusual, you might say. But we think the punishment fits your crimes."

Rosebud held herself very still. What in the world could it be?

"Here it is," Miss Arlotta finished up. "You have to be human."

"Human?" Rosebud barely had a chance to gasp, "How?" before Miss A leaned forward, raised her hand and clonked her right in the middle of the forehead.

Her arms flailing, Rosebud fell backward and just kept falling, right through the attic floor, through the third floor, the second and down into the lobby.

The first thing she hit was the hard wood and Oriental carpet in the lobby, right at the bottom of the main stairs. Flat on her back, she went splat, and it knocked the wind out of her. Her wire-rimmed glasses fell off her nose and made a small plink on the floor, and then, in rapid succession, two small, well-used books landed next to her, too. *Little Rosebud's Lovers* by Laura Jean

Libbey, and *Lady Audley's Secret* by Mary Elizabeth Braddon.

There were all kinds of people milling in the lobby, and every head turned her way. "Did she fall down the stairs?" someone asked. "What in the world is she wearing?"

"Rose?" She couldn't move yet, but then Ned was by her side, kneeling next to her and brushing her hair back from her face. He stared at her as if he couldn't believe she was real. "Rose? Thank God it's you."

She sat up halfway. "Ned?"

"How did you get here?" he asked quickly. "Are you all right? I've been looking for you everywhere! I didn't expect you to drop in my lap, but I'm not complaining. However you got here is fine by me."

She felt very strange. Kind of solid and heavy. She was definitely visible, since everyone there could see her, and yet she hadn't tried to materialize. She'd never before become visible without even trying.

She also felt very bare in her usual camisole, corset and bloomers. That, too, was a new feeling. Before she hadn't noticed much whether she had clothes on or not, although she knew it was important to Ned. But now she crossed her arms over her exposed breasts, blushing pink all over, and realized how much skin you could see through the thin linen and lace. A lot. It was both scary and exciting to gauge the heat in his gaze as he stared at her transparent clothing. Even if she could've done without everyone else in Maiden Falls gawking at her, too.

"What happened?" she asked, glancing around the lobby. "How did I get here?"

But then she remembered the trial in front of Miss

Arlotta. *The worst punishment we can think of... You have to be human....*

"Uh-oh," she whispered. She poked herself hard in the arm. She poked Ned, too, to see if it felt the same. "Ned, I got turned into a real person," she cried, grasping his shoulders, trying to scramble to her knees, trying to make it clear. "There was a trial and it was my punishment. I'm human!"

"I don't know what you're talking about," he told her, stripping off his jacket and wrapping it around her. "And I don't care. I called off the wedding, and I still want you. If you really think you're a ghost, well, we'll just deal with it. We'll just deal. Because I'm not losing you."

"You called it off?" she sputtered. There was so much to take in. And she felt so different now. So human. She pinched herself. She had skin. She had bones. She was solid. It was quite bizarre. "That's wonderful news. You're free, Ned. Free."

He stopped. Sounding perfectly logical, perfectly Ned, he said, "I could hardly marry her if I'm in love with you, could I?"

"No." She smiled. "No, you couldn't." But then she remembered the rest of what he'd said. "Ned, you don't have to deal with me being a ghost. I just told you I'm not one anymore. I'm human now."

"I don't care, Rose. That's the thing," he said with conviction. "Whatever it takes for you and me to be together, we will do it."

"You and me together," she echoed. "Is it possible?"

"I went to your hiding place in the attic but there was nothing there." Ned exhaled a shaky breath as he gathered her close. "I was so scared I would never find you again. I've never been so scared. What happened?"

"It's a long story. I got in big trouble for messing up so many things." She threw her arms around his neck and hugged him, reckless and unconcerned that his jacket had fallen off her arms. She needed to feel him as close as possible for a long moment.

Ned bent his head next to hers. He closed his eyes, and she could see his lips form the words "Thank you."

"I'm not going to muck things up like that anymore," she promised. "I'm going to do things right, Ned. I'm so sorry. About a lot of things. Especially knocking you out. When you didn't believe me, I didn't know what to do. But I realize now that I was wrong. I shouldn't have given you that shock."

"You're not going to do it again, are you?" He paused. "And your name really is Rose, isn't it? Or Rosebud?"

"It's Rose. Rose Elizabeth Tate." Rose gazed at his sparkling blue eyes, his perfect lips... She lifted her finger to his bottom lip. She couldn't believe how lucky she was to get to be here and see them and touch them in person, not as a ghost, not as an interloper, but because she *belonged.* "We have a lot of things to talk about, Ned. A lot of things to decide."

She realized suddenly that it was going to be strange living in the twenty-first century, with so many movies and books, so many things she hadn't experienced, so much trouble to get into, and...and Ned.

"You have to kiss me, Ned," she whispered. "That's how I know I belong."

Ned stood up, holding out a hand to draw her to her

feet, too. He settled the jacket more securely around her and even bent and picked up her books. She stood there, waiting, and then he clasped her in his arms and bent down to find her mouth. As he kissed her senseless, she looped her arms around his neck and kissed him with every bit of pent-up love and passion she'd been holding in for 109 years.

"I think I'm going to enjoy this," she murmured into his mouth. She felt his smile curve against hers. So right. So perfect.

Without a doubt, Rose knew she was finally in the right place at the right time.

Epilogue

A Sunday in June
Maiden Falls, Colorado, 2005

"NED, I'M NOT SURE this is a good idea," Rose tried again.

She'd been telling him the same thing all the way up the mountain, but he hadn't taken her objections seriously yet. The closer they got to the Inn at Maiden Falls, the more anxious she became. She couldn't put her finger on exactly what the problem was, but she had little alarm bells ringing in her ears, and they were getting louder.

Now, as Ned pulled the car into the parking lot, the alarm bells gave way to full-scale sirens.

"What, are you afraid you'll get stuck here again?" he asked. He reached over and took her hand. Raising it to his lips, he kissed her fingertips, and she felt the familiar sparks. His kiss always affected her that way. "Not a chance, Rose. I wouldn't let that happen. I'd just come and find you, that's all."

Rose shivered. "No one can ever know what fate has in store for them."

But as she gazed up at the pink Queen Anne mansion, not so different from the very first time she'd seen it, she began to feel more calm. She smiled. She always had liked the fact that it was pink. "How very cheery," she said out loud.

"What did you say?"

"Oh, it's nothing. Just what I thought to myself the very first time I saw Miss Arlotta's establishment. The house was painted pink and I thought that was cheery." It was funny she remembered that, especially since so many of her memories of her time here had faded. But that first day still remained clear. Such an impulsive, foolish girl she'd been, rushing off in a mad quest to become a harlot. She'd paid her penance for that mistake, many times over.

And yet now that she was here, with Ned, in a world that was incredibly more interesting and entertaining than her own, what with *Lord of the Rings* and whirlpool baths and Jimmy Choos and contact lenses and miniskirts and love—*especially* love—she wouldn't have changed a thing.

As she and Ned circled around the outside of the Inn, she mused, "I wonder if Miss Arlotta and the Judge and the girls are still in there. I wonder if they're looking out at us now."

It was strange how distant and vague her recollection of Miss Arlotta and the others had become, how years of memories could just trickle away. And yet that was exactly what had happened in the ten months since she'd landed in Ned's lap in the lobby.

They'd gone back to Denver, he'd somehow wrangled birth certificates and diplomas and a whole new identity for her as Rose Elizabeth Tate, born in 1974 instead of 1874, and no one seemed the wiser. She didn't know how he did it. Apparently Ned had some magic tricks of his own. Now people always told her she looked young for her age, which made her laugh. If they only knew.

She had enrolled in college for the fall, and she thought she might like to study literature, specifically sensational novels and dime novels of the late nineteenth and early twentieth centuries. She'd read them all the first time around, and she had given a lot of thought to the subject. *Little Rosebud's Lovers* by Miss Laura Jean Libbey would be first on her list. That Rosebud, the one in the book, had come to a very bad end, what with being seduced, abandoned, pursued, stalked and kidnapped, and dying at the age of sixteen. But this Rosebud was doing just fine, thank you.

With her college plans firm, she'd even agreed to marry Ned. It hadn't seemed right while she still wasn't sure who she was or where she was going, but Ned had managed to convince her she was exactly the same Rose she'd always been.

So they'd hosted a barbecue for as many of Ned's friends and relatives as they could cram into the backyard last week, and tied the knot right there, with a judge friend of Ned's presiding. No Westicotts invited. Ned's parents were present, however, and all was well on that front. Except for her own, Rose had always gotten along well with parents. Now that they were officially married, she and Ned planned to prolong the honeymoon as long as possible.

As far as she could tell, the mortal body she'd been given was in perfect health, it worked like anybody's else's, and she had finally, *finally* moved past twenty-one. She hadn't told Ned yet, but she thought her biological clock might even be ticking. No chance of Edmund John Mulgrew V, though. Mike, Susie, Buffy... Anything but Edmund.

For right now Rose was taking one step, one moment, at a time, embracing each and every exciting gift her new life offered. As long as she was with Ned, she knew she would be fine. Better than fine.

Ned steered her toward the front steps of the Inn, but Rose pulled back. "I'm not ready to go inside yet."

"It's been almost a year," he said gently. "I don't know about you, but I have good memories of this Inn. I met the love of my life here." He caught her around the waist and dropped a kiss on the top of her head. "It was the weirdest thing. This crazy little chambermaid popped up out of nowhere and kissed me and nothing has been the same since."

"You kissed me," she corrected.

"You have a terrible memory. *You* kissed *me.*"

"Okay, maybe you're right." Framing his face with her hands, staring into those gorgeous blue eyes, Rose reached up to find his lips one more time. She had such a hard time keeping her hands off him. "You know, it was when I kissed you that I knew. Even that first time."

"You knew that I loved you?"

"Yes. But also that we were meant to be, that there was something between us that I couldn't turn away from." She laughed. "Aren't you glad I was such a terrible misfit as a ghost?"

"Oh, yeah." Ned gathered her close and kissed her again, harder and deeper, paying no attention to the fact that more hotel guests had arrived behind them, and a bellman even came out to pick up luggage.

"Honeymooners," someone snickered. "This place is crawling with them."

Rose lamented, "Oh, Ned, we've turned into every other honeymoon couple that ever stayed here, all those sappy people I used to make fun of." She broke away from his embrace, pulling him down the steps. "I don't want to go inside. Let's take a walk through town instead. You know, I never made it down to the Falls. I got here that first Sunday, after they'd already had their Sunday picnic. And then I was stuck inside the house until I left with you. I want to see the Falls."

"Never could deny you anything," he grumbled, allowing himself to be dragged along behind his beautiful bride.

She wanted to taste Maiden Falls fudge and pizza and ice cream, and she absolutely insisted they stop at the souvenir shop so she could peruse the garters and the faux-pearl-handled toy pistols and snap up the T-shirts that proclaimed, The Spirits Are Always Willing In Maiden Falls.

"You don't want that T-shirt," he told her.

"Yes, I do. I love it." She wanted to wear it out of the store, but Ned convinced her that it wouldn't look right with her little black halter dress.

"You know, Ned," she began as they strolled down the main street of Maiden Falls. The sound of rushing water grew louder with every step, cluing them in that they were nearing the Falls. "The world has a lot of fun stuff in it. I'm so glad I got the chance to find that out."

"Me, too, Rose." His voice seemed to catch. "I don't know what I'd do without you."

"You are so adorable," she whispered. How was it possible to be this lucky?

She slipped off her shoes as they came to the park, digging her toes into the springy green grass. It felt wonderful. Ned automatically reached over and collected her shoes. He knew her well enough to realize she would probably lose them if he didn't, and she loved him for it. Ned kept her on track; she kept him off balance. They really were a perfect match.

With her arm linked through his, hugging him close, Rose didn't say anything, just gazed up at the roaring Falls. The water was white and clean, roaring down from the mountains, and she could almost feel the spray from here.

Rose smiled, taking in the majesty and grandeur of the Falls, rising high above the small park with its square of green grass and the tiny, perfect white gazebo. She blinked. For a second there...

She stood very still. Where there had been nothing a moment before, now shimmering, indistinct figures appeared before her. They were transparent and she could see the Falls and the gazebo through them, but they were definitely there.

One curvy woman, a stunning blonde wearing apricot silk, stretched out her legs on a picnic cloth, and then raised a glass of champagne, as if to toast Rose. She had long, pale hair, the color of cornsilk, wide blue eyes and a smile that lit up the whole park. Sunshine. Her old friend Sunshine.

There were others, too, maybe even Belle, in the

background, nestled close to the man with whom she'd climbed the stairs to the Great Beyond. And they had a little girl with them. Their daughter?

It was so lovely, so sweet, that Rose could hardly take it all in. But as quickly as they had appeared, the images vanished.

"Rose?" Ned waved a hand in front of her face. "You still here?"

"Yes. I think." She swallowed, her eyes still wide. "I think I just saw the Big Picnic in the Sky. I'm not sure. It was here and gone so fast. Maybe I just imagined it. But I think..."

"The Big Picnic in the Sky?" he echoed doubtfully.

"It doesn't matter." But she started to cry, overwhelmed with happiness and memories and too many emotions. Through her tears, she managed to choke out, "My friends are happy, Ned. You and I... We found bliss. And my friends are happy, too. Isn't it wonderful?"

"Aw, Rose, I know better than to try to understand the strange things that happen around you." He swept her up in his arms, carrying her and her shoes away from the park, away from the Falls, off to their future. "I guess that's what keeps life with you so entertaining."

On sale now

girls' night in

21 of today's hottest female authors
1 fabulous short-story collection
And all for a good cause.

Featuring *New York Times* bestselling authors

Jennifer Weiner (author of *Good in Bed*),
Sophie Kinsella (author of *Confessions of a Shopaholic*),
Meg Cabot (author of *The Princess Diaries*)

Net proceeds to benefit War Child, a network of organizations dedicated to helping children affected by war.

Also featuring bestselling authors...
Carole Matthews, Sarah Mlynowski, Isabel Wolff, Lynda Curnyn,
Chris Manby, Alisa Valdes-Rodriguez, Jill A. Davis, Megan McCafferty,
Emily Barr, Jessica Adams, Lisa Jewell, Lauren Henderson,
Stella Duffy, Jenny Colgan, Anna Maxted, Adèle Lang,
Marian Keyes and Louise Bagshawe

RED DRESS INK™

www.RedDressInk.com   www.WarChildusa.org

Available wherever trade paperbacks are sold.

™ is a trademark of the publisher.
The War Child logo is the registered trademark of War Child.

RDIGNIMMR

eHARLEQUIN.com

The Ultimate Destination for Women's Fiction

For **FREE online reading,** visit
www.eHarlequin.com now and enjoy:

Online Reads
Read **Daily** and **Weekly** chapters from
our Internet-exclusive stories by your
favorite authors.

Interactive Novels
Cast your vote to help decide how these
stories unfold...then stay tuned!

Quick Reads
For shorter romantic reads, try our
collection of Poems, Toasts, & More!

Online Read Library
Miss one of our online reads?
Come here to catch up!

Reading Groups
Discuss, share and rave with other
community members!

For great reading online,
visit www.eHarlequin.com today!

"Twisted villains, dangerous secrets…irresistible."
—*Booklist*

New York Times Bestselling Author

STELLA CAMERON

Just weeks after inheriting Rosebank, a once-magnificent Louisiana plantation, David Patin was killed in a mysterious fire, leaving his daughter, Vivian, almost bankrupt. With few options remaining, Vivian decides to restore the family fortunes by turning Rosebank into a resort hotel.

Vivan's dream becomes a nightmare when she finds the family's lawyer dead on the sprawling grounds of the estate. Suddenly Vivian begins to wonder if her father's death was really an accident…and if the entire Patin family is marked for murder.

Rosebank is not in Sheriff Spike Devol's jurisdiction, but Vivian, fed up with the corrupt local police, asks him for unofficial help. The instant attraction between them leaves Spike reluctant to get involved—until another shocking murder occurs and it seems that Vivian will be the next victim.

kiss them goodbye

"Cameron returns to the wonderfully atmospheric Louisiana setting…for her latest sexy-gritty, compellingly readable tale of romantic suspense."—*Booklist*

*Available the first week of October 2004,
wherever paperbacks are sold!*

Receive a FREE hardcover book from

HARLEQUIN ROMANCE®

in September!

Harlequin Romance celebrates the launch of
the line's new cover design by offering you
this exclusive offer valid only in September,
only in Harlequin Romance.

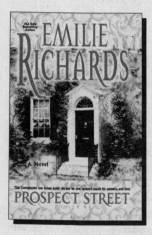

To receive your
FREE HARDCOVER BOOK
written by bestselling author
Emilie Richards, send us four
proofs of purchase from any
September 2004 Harlequin
Romance books. Further details
and proofs of purchase can be
found in all September 2004
Harlequin Romance books.

*Must be postmarked
no later than October 31.*

**Don't forget to be one of the first
to pick up a copy of the new-look
Harlequin Romance novels in September!**

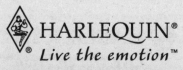

Visit us at www.eHarlequin.com

HRPOP0904

The world's bestselling romance series.

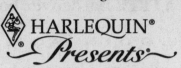

Seduction and Passion Guaranteed!

THEPRINCESSBRIDES

For duty, for money…for passion!

Discover a thrilling new trilogy from a rising star of Harlequin
Presents®, Jane Porter!

Meet the Royals…

Chantal, Nicolette and Joelle are members of the blue-blooded
Ducasse family. Step inside their sophisticated and glamorous
world and watch as these beautiful princesses find they have
to marry three international playboys—for duty, for money…
and definitely for passion!

Don't miss

THE SULTAN'S BOUGHT BRIDE (#2418)
September 2004

THE GREEK'S ROYAL MISTRESS (#2424)
October 2004

THE ITALIAN'S VIRGIN PRINCESS (#2430)
November 2004

**Pick up a Harlequin Presents® novel and you will enter a world
of spine-tingling passion and provocative, tantalizing romance!**

Available wherever Harlequin books are sold.

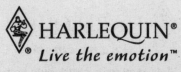